MR. S.O.B.

"I'm not sure I got what you said to me." Tim took a hard look at Jud.

"I said, 'You are a double-crossing son of a bitch.'"

"That's what I thought you said," Tim murmured. He moved toward Jud who took a step backward. Swiftly Tim drove his left fist into Jud's exposed belly.

The unexpected blow drove the breath from Jud with an explosive bray. Tim was on him like a cat. He spun Jud around and drove his left fist again through Jud's rising guard into his belly. Then came Tim's open-handed stinging slaps at Jud's face.

"You listenin'?" Tim asked quietly.

Jud nodded feebly.

"I don't mind being called a son of a bitch, but not by you. From now on you call me Mister Son of a Bitch."

THE STALKERS
LUKE SHORT

THE
STALKERS

by
Luke Short

BANTAM BOOKS · TORONTO · NEW YORK · LONDON

THE STALKERS
A Bantam Book / June 1973
2nd printing............October 1979

ISBN 0–553–12808–6

Published simultaneously in the United States and Canada

Bantam Books are published by Bantam Books, Inc. Its trade-
mark, consisting of the words "Bantam Books" and the por-
trayal of a bantam, is Registered in U.S. Patent and Trademark
Office and in other countries. Marca Registrada. Bantam
Books, Inc., 666 Fifth Avenue, New York, New York 10019.

COVER PRINTED IN THE UNITED STATES OF AMERICA
TEXT PRINTED IN CANADA

The Stalkers

1

The funeral of Mrs. Avery was held on an afternoon after the brief service. Dr. Rob Hasketh, who had attended her and watched her die, held back from the departing group as it scattered to the horses and buggies tied outside the cemetery at the edge of Driscoll.

When he saw Beth Avery step into the rented carriage along with three older women, he headed for his horse tied to the cemetery fence. He was a gangling, bespectacled man whose long face was much too serious for his thirty years, while his dark suit, appropriate for the occasion, seemed more for a hobbledehoy than for him.

Reaching his horse, he mounted and put the horse at a canter until he was in sight of the carriage. It pulled through the main street of town—four blocks of frame false-front buildings—turned left, and pulled up at the stopping block in front of a big, two-story, gray-painted frame house set among cottonwoods.

Chances were, the doctor thought, Beth would invite the women in for a cup of tea and listen to more condolences. However, Beth alone stepped from the carriage, halted, turned and waved, and the carriage pulled away. Touching heels to his horse's flanks, he rode up to the hitching post, dismounted, tied his horse, and headed up the walk toward the porch.

Beth climbed the steps, then halted and looked over her shoulder, hearing the sound of footfalls on the brick walk. Then she came back to the edge of the porch—a girl under average height, in a dress of navy

blue, a black straw hat with veil almost hiding a head
of lustrous black hair. As the doctor approached, she
used both hands to lift the veil and fold it back over
the brim of her hat. Her tear-reddened eyes were
pale gray, the corneas rimmed with a deeper blue
that was almost black. Her wide mouth, under a short
nose, drooped at the corners and there was a dark
stain under her eyes that more than hinted of what
she had been through.

Dr. Hasketh halted at the porch steps and he took
off his hat.

Beth said, "I'd like to be alone for a while, doctor."

"Yes, we've seen enough of each other these last
couple of weeks, haven't we? Still, spare me a minute,
if you will. This is important to you."

Beth sighed. She gestured to the two cane-bottomed
easy chairs in front of the porch swing. "Come, sit
down."

Beth moved over and seated herself in one of the
chairs. Dr. Hasketh followed and took the chair opposite her, placing his hat on the floor beside his chair.
He could look beyond her to the towering Rampart
Range whose foothills began immediately west of
town. It was his pleasure ofttimes to watch the drift-
ing clouds darken their already dark timber, but not
now.

Looking at her only, he asked then, "What's ahead
for you, Beth? Surely you've thought about it before
today."

She answered slowly. "Yes. There's this house and
no money left. I've thought I might hire a girl to help
me run a rooming and boarding house. I'm a good
cook."

He nodded. "You're a good nurse, too."

"Yes. First my father and then my mother. I should
be."

"If you decide on the rooming and boarding house,

I'm your first customer. But I was thinking of something else, too."

Beth regarded him with curiosity. "Isn't that enough?"

"You've got two big bedrooms off the kitchen." He paused, watching her frown, before he said, "Have you thought of a hospital, Beth?" As she opened her mouth in either surprise or protest he held up his hand, palm out, to silence her. "In the three months I've been here I've sent a half-dozen miners back to filthy bunkhouses, half of them to die. I've sent cowhands back to hog-wallow cow camps to pick up infections, all because there's no place to send them where they can be watched and cared for."

He spread his hands as if in quiet entreaty. "If you'll have me as a roomer, I'll be on call all day and here all night. I'd just like to try and save lives instead of helping to take them."

Beth was silent, pondering this, and the doctor went on. "As for pay, I'll get the mines and ranchers to guarantee your payment out of wages due. It should work, Beth, for both of us. And, God knows, it's needed."

"Will there really be enough patients to bother with?" Beth asked.

"Well, there's one on the cot in my office right now."

"Who is it?"

"I don't know; he doesn't know, either."

"What do you mean by that?" Beth demanded.

"Just what I said. He got a skull-splitting rap on the head by a bullet. He doesn't know who he is." The doctor picked up his hat and rose, then he said, "Think it over, Beth."

Dr. Hasketh turned in his horse to the hostler at Cannon's Feed Stable where his bay was boarded and headed up the main street boardwalk for his office.

He was sorry he'd had to brace Beth Avery about the hospital before her mother's grave was even covered over, but he thought he had done the right thing. At least, she now had hope and some notion of the shape of the future—very precious and necessary items in her present mood.

He halted before the frosted-glass door of his Main Street office, the same one that Beth's father had practiced from. He was wondering again about the lost man who was inside on the cot in the back room. When awake, he was perfectly normal, but he could remember nothing before being loaded onto a stage and being brought here.

On sudden impulse the doctor did not go inside, but instead headed upstreet for the county courthouse and the sheriff's office. Sheriff Will Davidson, whom he had seen but not talked to at the Avery funeral, had visited the hurt stranger this morning while Rob had been out on house calls. Had the sheriff learned anything new? the doctor wondered.

The county courthouse was two blocks upstreet, a corner two-story white-painted building housing the county offices on the ground floor and the Masonic Lodge on the second. On arriving, the doctor moved down the corridor between the county offices until he came to the last door on the left. A sign jutting out above the door, gilt letters on black, proclaimed, "County Sheriff."

Dr. Hasketh halted in the doorway. Sheriff Davidson's desk was in the rear corner, his chair facing the wall that held a gunrack supporting a dozen rifles and shotguns.

Sheriff Davidson had heard the footsteps and now slowly spun his swivel chair to face the door and his deputy's desk against the corridor wall. He was in his early forties—heavy, broad-shouldered, hair brushcut and blond as his full mustaches. He, too, was wearing a dark suit which gave him as little comfort as the doctor's suit allowed him.

Dr. Rob came in, nodded, and headed for the deputy's swivel chair which he swung around to face the sheriff, saying, "All funerals are too long," and sat down.

"Not for the preacher, though," the sheriff said dryly.

Dr. Rob asked abruptly, "What did you find out from the hurt man this morning, Will?"

"Next to nothing." The sheriff frowned. "He speaks like he's had some schooling. Where? He don't know. He reckons he has the average number of enemies, but not here or who'd want to follow him. In fact, he don't know a damn thing that's back of him, but he knows your name and the name of this town. Only because you told him, I reckon."

"Not who shot him?"

"No. He figures he was bushwacked. Even if they took everything from him except his clothes, he don't know why. Come to think of it he don't even know which way he was ridin', north or south. What do you reckon is the matter with him?"

"Amnesia. That's loss of memory from that shot that nicked him in the head."

"In a way, he's lucky," the sheriff growled. "There's plenty of things I wish I couldn't remember."

"How many people have you told that he's in my office, Will?"

"Hell, I don't know. It's no secret, is it? I reckon the stage-driver that picked him up has spread it all over town. Why?"

Dr. Rob took off his spectacles, pulled a handkerchief from his breast pocket and slowly began polishing the lenses. "Ever think that the man who tried to kill him might come back and finish the job? Especially if he knows where he is?"

The sheriff said slowly, "No, by God, I didn't. You think he might?"

"I just don't know." Dr. Rob then told the sheriff about his conversation with Beth Avery after the funeral concerning the use of two rooms of her house as the town's hospital. He finished by putting on his spectacles and saying, "Beth and a hired girl will be there all day. I'm taking a room there, so I'll be there at night. I think we should move him there and keep quiet about it. Right now, anybody could walk down my alley, poke out a windowpane, and kill him."

"Let's do it tonight, doc. I'll have a rig and we'll move him. I'll pick you up."

Dr. Rob left for his office feeling a vast sense of relief. There really was no safe way to protect his patient if someone wanted to kill him, but Beth's house was a lot safer than the office.

He let himself into his office, passed between his roll-top desk and an easy chair, walked through the break in the ceiling-high bookcases, skirted the examining table, and palmed the knob of the door that let into the back room. There was his own cot against the back wall; there was also a cot immediately to his left.

Standing beside it was a tall man dressed in Dr. Rob's own work shirt and levis. He held the doctor's pistol in his right hand and it was pointed at the doorway. Slowly, he lowered it, taking it off cock.

Dr. Rob asked, "Can you focus on me, friend?"

"On both of you," the man said wryly. He seemed to be in his early thirties and the bandage around his head just above the ears did not entirely cover his near-red straight hair. His wide-spaced green eyes under heavy eyebrows turned from chill to warm as Dr. Rob moved passed him and tossed his hat on the cot.

"Still dizzy?" Dr. Rob asked.

"Well, I'd rather sit down than stand. That's for sure."

"Then do it. I've got some news for you. Have you got any for me, like something you've remembered?"

The stranger tossed his gun on the cot, then eased himself into a sitting position. "Nope. Slept all afternoon, if that's news."

Dr. Rob sat down and regarded the nameless stranger. He was a ruggedly handsome man with an indefinable air of authority about him in spite of a week's growth of beard that blurred the angles of his lean face. His aquiline nose was slightly bent at the bridge, a token of some past brawl.

"We're moving out of this hole tonight, both of us." Dr. Rob explained the move to the Avery place and the reasons for it. "Beth can watch you and feed you. That's more than I can do. Suit you?"

"I'm broke, doctor. I don't even know where to write for money to pay."

"You will. Just take my word for it. Now let me look at my sew-up job on your head and change the bandage."

2

It was two o'clock Sunday morning and the parlor of the Widow Beaman's whorehouse held a dozen or so men waiting for more attractive girls than the one sitting on the stool at the corner of the small bar. She was well fleshed under her purple dress, not fat, with narrow, closely placed eyes and a slack mouth made more so by the whiskey she had been belting down most of the night. Her name was Pearl, and she was listening to a fancy-dressed whiskey drummer tell a story to three other men bellied up to the bar:

"This happened in Dodge. A man that saw it told me. A fellow bet fifty dollars with the prettiest girl in the house that she wouldn't walk mother-naked down the middle of the street a block and back. In daylight. She took him up, but under these conditions: she would do it at first light and she would carry a gun. She would shoot any son of a bitch that looked at her. Her words, and the bet was on."

"What happened?" one of the drinkers asked.

"She did it and won her bet," the drummer said.

The men at the bar laughed mildly, believing it was only a drummer's yarn.

Pearl's voice broke into the laughter. "God, that's the easiest fifty dollars a girl could earn."

The men looked at her and, almost as one, looked at the stocky, broad-faced drummer. He in turn looked at Pearl, ran a thumb over his pencil-thin mustache, smiled, and said, "I'll make you the same bet, girlie."

8

Pearl's eyes focused on the drummer. "You mean it?"

For answer, the drummer reached in his hip pocket, brought out a snap purse, opened it, and emptied the contents into his hand. He sorted out two double eagles and an eagle and laid them on the counter, then looked at Pearl. "There's mine. Where's yours?"

The uniformed Negro maid who was acting as bartender leaned against the back bar, folded her arms across her enormous breasts, and said, "You're drunk, Pearl."

"Not too drunk to walk two blocks," Pearl said. She rose, said, "I'll be back," and went through the curtained doorway into the corridor that the girls' rooms let on to.

The drummer said to the maid, "You're the stakeholder, Jessie," and shoved the coins across the bar. Jessie took a glass from the back bar, put the coins into it and said, "Widow Beaman ain't goin' to like this."

"She'll never know it happened until afterwards," the drummer said.

Pearl returned with her money. She was also carrying a pistol which she put alongside the money glass. "Like that other girl, I'm going to shoot any son of a bitch that looks at me naked." She gave Jessie a roll of bills and watched her put them in the glass which she placed on the back bar. "Now give me a drink, Jessie."

The drummer said, "If you pass out it's my money —all of it."

"I won't pass out," Pearl said scornfully. "I threw up back there."

The drummer put some money on the counter, said to Pearl, "I'll be back before daylight. And there's one man that's going to look at you and you better not shoot at him." He tapped his chest. "Me. I'm going to make damn sure you walk that block."

"All right. You've already seen me naked."

"That I have," the drummer said. "See you all later."

He went out just as a girl and a man came into the room from behind the curtain. The drummer shut the door, paused on the landing to chuckle soundlessly, and then took to the stairs. Once in the deserted street he walked out into the middle of it, turned, and looked up at the windows of the room he had just left. The shades were pulled. Even if someone were looking out he knew he could not be seen in the darkness.

Angling down the street, he headed for a two-story frame house wedged between two stores. There was a lamp in the bay window and as he went up the short walk he could hear the tinkling of a piano inside. Horses and buckboards were motionless at the tie rail in front of the house. He mounted the steps and went in without knocking.

Just as false dawn was breaking, he left the house. The horses and buckboards had vanished. Even as he moved down the walk of Queenie Billings's whorehouse the lamp in the bay window was blown.

He crossed the street and turned left. Hugging the storefronts so he could not be seen from Widow Beaman's second floor, he reached the steps, climbed them and entered the parlor.

Pearl was seated with two other girls at a table closest to a street window. She was wearing a wrapper as were the other girls. Five men, three of them the men the drummer had talked to earlier, were playing poker at the big corner table. They grinned at him and he grinned back, and then he spotted the gun on the table in front of Pearl.

The drummer walked over to the table, looked at Pearl, then at the gun. Pointing to it, he asked Pearl, "You know how to shoot that thing?"

Pearl nodded toward the table of men. "They showed me."

The drummer reached out for the gun and picked it up, asking, "Is it loaded?"

"You're damn right, all ready to go. Six shells," Pearl said, her speech slurred. She had been leaning on the whiskey since he left, he judged. He looked at the gun, said quietly, "Oh, Jesus," pointed the gun away from the table, aimed it at the floor and, braking the hammer with one hand, let the hammer down. It had been on full cock.

"I'll keep this till you start down the street." He went over to the bar and ordered a whiskey from a drowsy Jessie. While she was pouring it he glanced back at the girls. Pearl had her chair tilted back and had pulled the shade back.

"It's time," she called to him.

The drummer walked over to a window and raised the shade. It was gray outside in the empty street. He shook his head and said, "The deal was full daylight."

Going back to the bar, he sipped at his whiskey.

"Widow Beaman won't like this," Jessie said for the second time.

"Who's it hurt?" the drummer countered.

"Well, it just ain't proper."

"That's up to Pearl, not the widow."

He looked at Pearl and saw she was rising slowly, unsteadily. "It's daylight," she called to him. "I'm goin'."

The drummer looked at the window, saw she was right, picked up the gun, finished his whiskey and then headed for the door, where Pearl was waiting.

"Just look at the road, honey," one of the girls called.

Pearl and the drummer went out. As soon as the door closed, the men went around blowing out the lamps and raising the shades. From behind the net curtains they could not be seen from the street.

The drummer put a hand on Pearl's elbow and they

slowly descended the stairs together. At the bottom landing, Pearl unbelted her wrapper, dropped it and, standing naked, held out her hand for the gun. The drummer cocked it and handed it to her, butt first.

"When you pull that trigger it goes off," he said.

"What's on the street?" Pearl asked.

The drummer looked both ways around the corner of the doorway. "Nothing. It's empty. Get going."

As she passed him he slapped her rump and she giggled.

The drummer, watching her walk in the middle of the street and turn, decided she was all girl and no mistaking it. He waited and saw her pull even with Queenie's, the gun hanging from her right hand.

Suddenly, bedlam shattered the morning stillness and it came from Queenie's. Pans were being beaten. There were whistles and laughter and hoots.

"Hey, your muff's showing, Pearl!" a girl shrieked from the now-open bay window.

"Cover those two puppies, honey!" a man shouted.

Pearl halted, stunned. She turned, put her back to the house, and a man shouted, "Turn around, Satchel-butt!"

Pearl whirled to face the house, beginning a step toward it. Then her gun went off, not even pointed. She completed her step and her knees gave way. She fell heavily into the dusty street, and then her wild screams began, regular as drumbeats.

The drummer watched it all. He was laughing until she fell and the screams began. Quickly, he picked up her wrapper from the steps and ran across the boardwalk, ducked under the tie rail, and headed for Pearl.

He was not the first to reach her. Two men and a girl ran out of Queenie's and halted beside Pearl, whose screams were somewhat muted now.

The drummer pulled up and they all regarded Pearl's foot, which was torn and bleeding into the dust. The drummer handed Pearl's wrapper to the girl and said, "Get it on her and we'll turn her over." To one of the men he said, "Go in and get a clean towel."

Between the girl and the drummer they got Pearl's arms in the sleeves of the wrapper. It wasn't difficult since Pearl had fainted. By the time the man returned with the towel, Pearl was covered and Queenie herself, who was an old hag, plus the male customers, were gathered in the street.

The drummer wrapped the towel around her shattered and bleeding foot, then rose, looked around the group, and said bitterly, "Some bet."

"She knew what she was doin'," a man said.

"Not quite," the drummer replied. He looked around again. "You know the town and I don't. Who's the doc and where is he?"

A man said, "Doc Hasketh. He lives in the Avery house. Got a new hospital there."

The drummer nodded. "All right. When I asked you boys to move your horses around back, there were a couple of buckboards here. Is there still one?"

"Mine," a man said. "I'll bring it around," and he left.

In a few minutes they had Pearl loaded in the buckboard and covered with a blanket. The drummer climbed up beside the driver and they drove off, turning at the corner for Main Street. In another five minutes they turned into Avery's alley and halted the team by the kitchen porch.

The drummer was climbing the back-porch steps when the back door opened and Beth, in a gray wrapper buttoned up to her throat, stepped out.

The drummer yanked off his hat and said, "We've got a hurt girl out here. Is the doc here?"

Beth looked beyond him, saw Pearl, and then said, "Yes, I'll wake him. You follow me."

She turned and went back into the kitchen, walked

over to the door on her right, and opened it, the drummer behind her. There was a Mexican girl at the big black stove against the kitchen's front wall. Two beds and a dresser managed to almost fill the room she went into. She walked across the room, closed and locked the door to the adjoining room, then came back to the nearest bed, and folded down the covers.

"Bring her in here. I'll go get the doctor."

The drummer went out and Beth moved past the squat, almost square Mexican girl, opened the back-stairs door and climbed them. In the upper hall she paused before the closed door and knocked sharply.

"Yes," a sleepy voice mumbled.

"You have a woman patient in the bedroom, doctor."

"Be right down."

Beth went down into the kitchen. One of the two men was just closing the back door. Beth looked into the bedroom, heard the girl moaning, saw she was in bed, then went to the back door and opened it.

The drummer and his companion were talking by the buckboard. They fell silent at sight of this slight, black-haired, pretty girl as she moved out to the middle of the porch and said, "I'd like to talk to one of you."

The men looked at each other; the drummer shrugged then and moved to the steps and climbed them, again with hat in hand.

When he halted in front of Beth, she asked, "What happened to her?"

The drummer eyed her with resignation. "You won't like it, miss."

"Maybe not, but I want to hear it."

The drummer eyed her speculatively and then said, "Well, she's one of the Widow Beaman's fancy girls, if you know what I mean."

"I know what you mean. She's a whore. That's a

correct word. Why don't you say it?" She paused and the drummer blushed. "Did you hurt her?"

"No, nothing like that." Then he told of the bet, not sparing himself. Beth listened calmly as he told of making the dawn appointment with Pearl, then going over to Queenie's and tipping off the girls and their customers as to what was coming. He finished by saying, "She didn't know guns and she was full of booze that I didn't buy her. She was surprised and— and I guess mad. Anyway, she shot herself in the foot."

Beth looked at him with the utmost contempt. "So you didn't hurt her. Who did, if you didn't?"

"She hurt herself," the drummer said adamantly. "She's a lazy, greedy and stupid whore, or she wouldn't earn money the way she does!"

Beth nodded. "All true, probably. Still, you've got a strange sense of humor. I'm glad I don't know you."

She turned and started for the door when the drummer said to her back, "Look, miss. I won that bet with her, but I don't want the money. I'll bring it around to pay you and the doc."

Beth turned and said to him, "You do that. Maybe it'll help pay for a wooden leg if that foot has to come off."

She went inside.

The nameless man in the room behind the locked door of the room next to Pearl's finished his breakfast, put the tray on the night table between the two beds, then stretched hugely. He heard his nightgown rip at the armpit and swore softly. This was Dr. Rob's transferred patient. His green eyes at the moment held a look of barely controlled patience.

There was a knock on the hall door now and he called, "come in."

The door opened to admit Cruz, the Mexican girl,

and she was followed by Beth who exchanged good mornings with him. Beth had changed to a dark long-sleeved dress over which she wore an apron. She stepped aside as Cruz carried the tray out of the room and vanished, then seated herself at the foot of the bed. "Sleep well?" she asked.

"After I got used to that noisy hoot owl down the street."

"Has your name come back to you?" At the negative shake of his head, Beth asked gently, "Why don't you make one up for yourself? We have to call you something."

He smiled, revealing big, even white teeth. "Never thought of that. Will Jim do?"

"You think that might be your real name?"

He thought a moment. "It might be. It's the first name I thought of, but I can't think of anything that goes with it."

"All right. I'll give you your last name." She studied his face and again noticed the pale scar on the bridge of his nose. "You look as if you'd been in your share of fights. What about Battles for a last name?"

He laughed soundlessly. "Jim Battles. Why not?"

"That'll do until you remember your real one." She paused. "The doctor said I was to pester you with questions until you wouldn't hold still for more. Is that all right?"

"You go right ahead, m'am."

Beth leaned back against the footboard and asked, "Why were you headed for Driscoll?"

"Don't recollect I was."

"Anyplace beyond Driscoll—south, let's say?"

"Don't know of any place south of here. Mexico's got to be."

Beth pounced. "Ever been to Mexico?"

He scowled and said after a while, "If I have, I don't remember it."

"How'd you make a living, Jim? Were you a cowman? I ask that because of the clothes Cruz washed for you yesterday."

"Yes, I was."

"Any particular brand you remember?" Beth persisted.

Out of the corner of her eye she saw a movement in the hall and looked through the doorway to see Dr. Hasketh standing motionless, hands on hips. He smiled at her and came into the room. "I was eavesdropping, Beth. You're going good."

The doctor looked at his patient. "We've got a cowman on our hands, have we?"

"Name of Jim Battles," Jim said.

"Yours or made up?"

Jim grinned. "Made up. At least I remembered it."

"You remember everything that happened since you were brought into town. That means your brains weren't shot out, Jim. The rest will come."

"I remember someone moaning next door, too."

"Yes, a girl shot herself in the foot." He looked at Beth. "I gave her plenty of laudanum and cleaned up the foot. It's a mess. If it doesn't get infected and she doesn't lose it she might walk again. Just might. She missed the arch, but it's still a mess."

The doctor moved past Beth and halted by the night table, facing Jim. His glance strayed to the night table and he saw the sixgun lying on it.

"Why the gun?" he asked Jim.

"I don't know who shot me. If he hears I'm in this place, he might try to finish the job."

"Yes. You remembered that, too." The doctor looked back at Beth. "Can you leave us alone, Beth? I'm going to see if Mr. Jim Battles can walk, and he's got on a mighty short nightshirt."

3

Mahaffy Station lay fifteen miles from Driscoll by the tortuous stage road. Its location had been hacked out of the thick pine timber a few miles below the pass through the Ramparts.

To the innocent eye of a stage traveler stretching his legs while awaiting a team change, it was scarcely worth giving a name. Still, since it had a box-sized post office in a back corner of its log general store, it had required one.

Again, the innocent eye would have wondered mildly what the two-story log house close to the store could be. Not a hotel for travelers, for no sign proclaimed it. Aside from the blacksmith shop across the road from the store, with two large corrals and a barn behind it, there were a half dozen or so weathered log shacks facing each other across the road. Off to the north at the edge of the clearing there was an open-sided shed sheltering a sawmill.

A not-so-innocent eye would have observed more detail. Why did five men in worn range clothes, two of them obviously drunk, leave the store together as the stage was braking for its stop? Why did three of them head for the door of the two-story house, while the other two went to a mean shack up the street, knocked, and were admitted by a girl in a gaudy yellow dress? The tie rail in front of the store was empty. Where were the men's horses? If two men were drunk, where had they gotten their liquor, since there was no outward sign of a saloon?

18

The stage-driver had the innocent eye, or rather the incurious one. He had only one thing in mind. That was liquor, and he knew where to get it.

He had crossed the dusty road and climbed the two steps to the store's long porch before the blacksmith and his helper could come out to unhook the tired teams. Skirting one of the dozen barrel chairs scattered on the dusty porch, he went into the store, turned immediately left, and was in a one-room saloon, with a short bar on the right and two circular card tables under the twin high-set windows.

A slim, heavily bearded black-haired man rose from his seat at the far table on which some papers were scattered, said, "'Morning, Gus," and went behind the bar. He was over forty but moved with the lazy grace of a cat. The tall, leathery-complexioned driver tossed the mail sack on the bar top, said, "How's it today, June?" and watched June set a bottle of whiskey and a glass on the bar in front of him.

"Looks like you'll be in mud before you hit the pass."

"Yes, Goddamnit," Gus said with disgust. He poured out half a glass of whiskey, put it down in two breath-holding swallows, then refilled the glass to its top.

June laid a cigar beside the bottle, reached in the pocket of his vest for a match to put beside it, then leaned both his hands on the bar edge. "What's new in the big city, Gus?" Only then did he see the mail sack and reach for it.

Gus fired up the cigar while June picked up the mail sack and emptied its contents on the bar. A half-dozen letters fluttered to the bar top.

He was ramming them in his hip pocket as Gus chuckled. "Well, one of Widow Beaman's girls shot herself in the foot." He went on to tell of the bet, of the ambush at Queenie's and Pearl's shooting her foot, and finished by saying, "By God, I wish I'd seen that."

"Hurt bad?"

"I reckon. The doc's got her in the hospital."

"What hospital? In Driscoll?"

"Sure enough. The big Avery house. Beth Avery's turned it into a hospital. The new doc, he lives there now. She's takin' in roomers and boarders, too."

June scratched his cheek through his beard, making a burring sound, and said, "She won't make eatin' money on no hospital. On roomers, maybe, but not that."

"I dunno. She's full now, though."

"Anybody I'd know?"

"Well, there's Pearl and a woman havin' a baby. In the other room there's a miner with the DT's strapped in bed. There's another fellow in with him got shot in the head north of town. He don't even remember his own name. He don't know where he come from or where he was goin'. They found him on the road—no horse, no money, nothin' but what he was wearin'." Gus drank deeply.

"On the road?" June asked.

Gus swallowed his whiskey, nodding. "Right in the middle of it, they say. Hell, if I was goin' to rob a man and kill him, I'd damn well haul him out of sight." He picked up the mail sack, reaching in his pocket for money, as he always did.

And, as June said three times every week, he now said, "Hell, forget it."

"Thankee, June. You got anything goin' west?"

"I'll get it."

June came around the bar and went through the store, passed a man clerk, and went into the tiny post office. He picked up two letters, retraced his steps, gave the letters to Gus, and walked out to the edge of the porch.

He watched Gus climb up into the box, accept the reins from the hostler, and the stage was under way, headed for the cloud-shrouded pass.

The hostler started back for the blacksmith shop when June called, "Roy! Over here."

The young hostler reversed directions, crossed the road, and halted at the foot of the steps.

"Remember those two horses I brought in five—six days back?" At Roy's nod June went on, "Take 'em up to Willow Springs and turn 'em loose."

"Hell, that's close to Tyler's. They'll get stolt, sure as you're born."

"That's what I'm hoping," June said dryly. "Saddle up my dun and tie him here before you take off."

He turned and went back into the bar and sat down before the papers he had left. He brushed them aside carefully and said softly, "Son of a bitch."

June (for Junior) Constable was now in the bind of his life, he knew. Ten years ago, when he'd been on the run with two saddlebags of loot he'd taken at gunpoint from a bank, he saw Mahaffy Station in time to duck his horse into the timber. Tying his horse well away from the road, he'd walked back to watch the tiny settlement. Less than an hour later, he'd seen five heavily armed riders, coming from the same direction he'd come, pull up at the store's tie rail and file inside the store. While they were inside, a stage pulled in from the west for a team change and he laughed out loud. If they'd been following his sign they'd lost it to the west and would soon lose it again to the east, since the stage teams would take care of both. Three of them took to the porch chairs and began eating what they'd bought inside; the other two crossed the road to talk to the stage-driver, who was talking to the blacksmith. "No, nobody has passed through here or we'd have seen him," the blacksmith was probably saying. "No, I didn't meet nobody except a man driving a team and that was 'way back," the stage-driver was saying, June had guessed.

During the next half hour and after the stage pulled out, he studied Mahaffy Station very carefully. What a place to work out of, he thought. It was remote and unknown, except to the local cattlemen, the stage-drivers, and maybe a few people in the town below.

When the five sought their horses and headed back the way that they'd come, he went back to his horse and rode south through the thick timber until he came to water. He followed it upstream until he rode into a clearing that held some grass because the sun could reach it. He unsaddled, staked out his horse to graze the meager grass, then sought the biggest pine at the edge of the clearing. Long before dark he had dug a hole at its base and buried the two saddlebags. He did not blaze this tree with his knife, but he did peel off a great swatch of bark from a tree four trees away from it. Then he made a cold camp, ate some jerky hidden in his bedroll, and then rolled into his blankets.

Next morning he'd put a small stone in one of his boots before pulling it on. He walked around and found he couldn't keep from limping, which was exactly what he had wanted.

He had saddled up and rode upstream. When he was certain he was beyond Mahaffy Station, he turned north, picked up the road, and was soon dismounted in front of the store. He limped inside and looked around under the sour gaze of an old white-haired man. He introduced himself, said he was so crippled up from a horse falling on him, he'd had to sell his ranch and was looking for easier work. Would Mahaffy consider selling?

The old man looked surprised that someone should ask such an idiot question. Of couse, he'd sell. His "rumatiz" was murdering him and he wanted to live in town. He owned everything here. When he mentioned the price, June said he had half of that. Mahaffy agreed on half, the other half to come, and they shook hands on the deal. June knew he had more than that in the buried saddlebags. In that first long conversation he learned that the station was not in the same county as Driscoll and that in all the years Mahaffy had been here the law had come only once in search of a fugitive.

After Mahaffy and his old lady moved out, June went over the pass to Corbett, the county seat of Mineral County. Here, he hired a bookkeeper clerk who had been fired for stealing from his employer and his fourteen-year-old grandson.

It took him somewhat longer to find a woman that suited him. He tried bringing out whores from Corbett, but this dead and dismal backwash depressed and frightened them. One spent three days, two of them drunk in the saloon, before she left on the stage to Corbett.

It was only four months later that he found his woman, or rather she found him. It was on the stagecoach from the north headed for Corbett. It took two minutes for him to guess correctly that she was a whore from nowhere going nowhere. She had lost her looks and she was sick. Her cough rumbled like the coach she was riding in.

"Where you bound for?" he had asked her.

"I don't know."

"What do you mean, you don't know?"

She had given a searing cough that almost gagged her. Under control again she had said, "I kept ten dollars and gave the station agent the rest. I told him I wanted to go south as far as that would take me."

June had regarded her a long time before he said, "You're crazy."

"I know I am," she had answered calmly.

"How are you goin' to live once you're where you're goin'?"

"The way I've lived since I was twelve. Off men."

"That can't last forever."

"Neither can I, thank God."

June had guessed her age at between thirty-five

and forty. Here she was—up for grabs, broke, certainly sick and friendless. He thought of his own lonely circumstances, which were better than hers.

He had said then with his usual brutal candor, "What can you do besides climb into bed with a man for money?"

She took this without flinching. "What most women do, you son of a bitch. I can cook, keep a clean house, wash clothes, sew, raise chickens and a garden and babies."

"Then why aren't you doin' those things instead of pickin' up strangers on a train?"

"I've done them all and lost them all," she had said flatly. "Anyway, why do you care?"

"How'd you like to be my aunt? You're old enough to be."

She had regarded him thoughtfully, then asked, "Now who's crazy?"

He had told her then who he was and how he lived off a small store and saloon out in the backbrush. He needed a woman to bring some order and comfort into his life, but without marriage and without having to whore with other men. She could pass as his aunt. She would keep his house and be in all ways a wife to him. Eventually, he would be well off. She would never need for money, food, or shelter. It was a fair trade, he had told her. Security for her, a housekeeper-mistress for him.

Not unsurprisingly, she agreed. She had turned out to be a good-hearted, undemanding woman, utterly silent about her past, content with the present and unworried about the future. She took good care of their house, tried to keep him cleaner than he wanted to be, and managed their money with care.

That first winter he must have written a hundred letters to about a dozen men he'd known in prison and were now out. He informed them he was organizing a wild bunch to hold up trains, banks and mines, or anything else. They would headquarters here; if that didn't suit them then come here on the first Monday of every other month. He would have a job set up for them. They would pull it off, scatter afterward, and meet here until things cooled off. Six of them accepted by spring; they had been successful, too. They traveled far and separately, meeting only for the action and separating afterward. Over the nine years they operated, two had been killed but none captured, and June was getting rich.

It was one of the original six, now married and a deputy sheriff in a northern county, who wrote the letter June had before him now. He'd got it a week ago.

June:
Better watch out. A deputy U.S. Marshal stopped by the office today. Wanted to know how to get to Mahaffy Station. Told him I didn't know, but he'll find out somewhere. Both horses branded Circle 6. He's big, green eyes, kind of red hair, likely thirty. I figure he's got a four-day ride to Driscoll. Got to get this on the stage south. Get him before he gets you.

Dock

June wadded up the letter, rose, went over to the cold stove, threw the letter into it, then walked back behind the bar and poured himself a whiskey and drank it. *Get him before he gets you,* Dock had written. Well, he'd tried, but according to Gus this Marshal Tim Sefton was alive in Driscoll's new hospital, hurt enough he couldn't even remember his name. Well, after shooting him off his horse, June had carried him away from the road, taken everything he had on him, including his wallet and identifying papers and badge, so nobody in town knew his name either.

June poured another, smaller drink and put his elbows on the bar. Why in hell hadn't he shot him again? He knew. There was already a hole in his head that was bleeding a bucket of blood. Then there were the two horses branded Circle 6 and his own horse to move off the road out of sight before somebody came along and got curious.

There was only one thing to do now, and he'd known it as soon as Gus finished talking. He had to go down to Driscoll and finish the job he'd bungled.

4

Since June had always made a point of avoiding Driscoll, he could be reasonably sure he wouldn't be recognized on this bright and sunny morning by anyone there.

The town was astir and the saloons open for the early drinkers. Putting in at the tie rail fronting a Main Street café, he went inside. At dark last night he'd made a cold camp and ate some biscuits before rolling into his blankets, so he was hungry now.

It was a family-style café here with two long tables whose chairs were almost filled with working men, cowhands, and clerks. Huge platters of steaks and potatoes, bread and butter, were spotted at intervals in the middle of the tables. June found a chair and helped himself to all the food he could eat.

A middle-aged waitress, a huge coffeepot in her hand, made a constant patrol of the tables, filling the cup of whoever held one up. She was pleasant and seemed to know most of her customers. In her third time around, June, finished with breakfast, held up his cup. As she filled it, he said, "Hear tell you got a new hospital here."

"Yep," she chuckled. "Just in time for me."

"Where's it at?"

"The Avery place."

"I'm new here. Where's that?"

She pointed with her free hand. "End of this block, turn right and two blocks over. Big gray house you can't miss."

"I see." June rose, paid the woman behind the desk at the door, and went out.

Following directions, he identified the house on his left next to the corner house. Watching the house, he observed several things about it: smoke was coming from the chimney, so the occupants were awake; there was a side door near the rear on the north side; there was a discreet sign, black on white, nailed to the porch rail, proclaiming, "Room and Board."

As he went left at the corner, he thought, *No hospital sign. No they wouldn't need that, but that's where it is.* There was a white-painted church on the corner to his right.

At the alley that divided the block, he again turned his horse left, wanting a look at the back of the house. What he saw was a big back porch and two tall ground-floor windows, widely separated. He passed a big gray-painted shed and rode on. If this Beth Avery was watching her pennies, and she obviously was, she'd be doing the grocery-buying herself for the six people she had to feed, he reasoned. She'd also have to get help for the cooking, housework, and patient-watching, so that meant she likely had a woman to help her.

At the mouth of the alley he put his horse right, went around the half block, and turned into the alley behind the church. An open-faced shed ran the width of the church property for the shelter of the horses and vehicles of the worshippers. He put his horse under the shelter, moved past the far side of the church, sought the front steps, and sat down on the top one. He was careful to limp up them. From here, he could see the porch and walk of the Avery house.

He had to wait an hour before he saw a man, carrying a small black bag, and a slight young woman dressed in green come down the steps of the Avery house together and take the brick walk leading to Main Street. The doc, for sure. Beth Avery? Maybe.

He waited until they were into the next block, then went down the steps and crossed the street to the alley behind the Avery house. Turning at the gray shed, he moved up to the back porch, climbed the steps and knocked on the door. It was opened by a squat Mexican girl.

"*Buenas dias, señorita,*" June said, touching his hat-brim.

Glad to be spoken to in her own language, Cruz said, "*Buenas dias, señor. Como le va?*"

In fluent Spanish, June said, "Fine, thank you. I am looking for the new hospital. Could this be it?"

"Surely," Cruz said. "Are you sick or hurt?"

June smiled and shook his head. "Nothing like that. Do you have a miner in here for a patient?"

Cruz nodded cautiously.

"I'd like to see him. He worked for me and I owe him money. A good man, if he didn't drink so much."

"A nice old one, Señor 'Artman." She looked at him closely. "You don't bring him whiskey, I hope."

"No." He opened his duck jacket and spread it wide to show her he concealed no bottle. "Whiskey will kill him and I like the old man."

Cruz smiled. "He is better, but not strong yet."

She was about to invite him inside when she realized he should not go through the room with the women in it. She put up a hand to halt him, then walked past him to the edge of the porch. Pointing, she said, "Around the corner there is a door. Go through it into a hall. Turn left—" she hooked her arm and wrist to the left— "then there is a door on the right. You'll find him there."

June thanked her. She smiled and then June slowly limped down the steps and turned left. She was watching him from the doorway, but when he looked back at her she went into the kitchen.

As June approached the two big windows, he bent over so that he could not be seen from inside. Round-

ing the corner he opened the door to the hall, left
it open, turned left, and tiptoed down to the open
doorway on the right.

An old man in his long underwear was standing
at the foot of the bed. By the time he was aware of
June, June had knocked loudly on the doorframe and
said, "Hello, Hartman. What in hell are they doing
to you?"

June stepped into the room, hand in jacket, heading
for the old man. Then, as if he had just realized
there was another bed in the room, he halted and
looked at Marshal Sefton sitting up in bed.

June's hand came out of his pocket with the gun,
just as Sefton threw his pillow. It caught June full in
the face, blinding him and clinging for the second it
took the marshal to roll between the beds.

June clawed the pillow away from his face, located
the marshal and snapped a shot without aiming. The
marshal had a gun in his hand and he shot now. June
felt the slug slam into his shoulder with such violence
that his reflex popped the gun out of his hand onto
the floor, and half-turned him back toward the doorway. Frantically, he lunged for the doorway. The
marshal's second shot slammed into the doorframe by
his head, and then he was in the hall, running for the
open door. Once outside, he turned toward the street
and ran across the two yards, headed for his horse,
already holding his shoulder.

Inside the room, Jim came to his feet, started for
the door, lost his balance and sprawled on his belly.
He lay there for seconds, the room spinning. Old Hartman, who had dropped to the floor at June's first
shot, came slowly to his feet, went up to Jim, leaned
over him and asked, "You hurt, fella?"

"Just dizzy," Jim answered. "Can you help me
up?"

At that moment Cruz, out of breath, halted in

the doorway, saw Jim sprawled on the floor, gun in hand, and screamed.

"Be quiet, girl. He's all right. Help me get him in bed."

Cruz was still tearful when Beth returned. When Cruz heard the front door open, she ran; through the dining room, sobbing again, and in the living room she threw herself into Beth's arms. Half-choking, she blurted out her story. She had let the bearded stranger into the bedroom because he was a friend of Mr. Hartman. She'd only wanted to cheer up the old man. Instead, the stranger had shot at Mr. Battles, who had shot back. No, Mr. Battles hadn't been hit.

Beth hugged her and said, "It's all right, Cruz. You were trying to help. Now stop crying."

Beth hurried across the room to the side hall and before she reached Jim's room she was almost running, smelling powdersmoke. She knocked on the door, opened it and looked at Jim, who was lowering his gun. "Cruz told me. Are you really all right, Jim?"

"Good as ever," he answered. He was wearing the bathrobe Dr. Hasketh had loaned him. Now he said, "I want to talk to you alone, Beth. Why don't we go into the living room?"

"If you can make it."

"Just stay beside me." He climbed out of bed, half-waved to Hartman in the other bed, and Beth stepped to his side. Together they went down the hall, Jim hugging the wall. In the living room, Beth put a hand on his elbow, steadying him, and they crossed to the sofa against the front wall. Jim sat down carefully; only then did Beth move to one of the two easy chairs facing the sofa and sit down. "Was it the same man that shot you?"

"I don't remember him, but it has to be. Who else wants me dead?"

Beth couldn't disguise her shiver as she asked in an uncertain voice, "Oh, Jim, what do we do? You can't have any peace ever if you fear every stranger."

"Not every stranger—only ones with a right arm in a sling." At Beth's look of bewilderment, he said, "I shot him in the upper right arm or shoulder." He grinned. "That cuts it down considerable."

Beth only shook her head, not comforted. Jim said then, "Beth, you won't like this, but I'm getting out of here." When Beth opened her lips to protest, Jim silenced her with a gesture. "Whoever's hunting me knows I'm here now. He'll be back, or send somebody to finish the job. He'll shoot you or Cruz or doc to get to me. He's got to have me dead."

"But why, Jim! Why!"

"I wish I knew," Jim answered gloomily.

"Have you ever killed a man, Jim?"

Jim was silent, frowning, then he said, "It's no good, Beth. I just don't know. Maybe I've killed a dozen men. That's what I wonder about. If I hadn't, why would any man want to kill me?"

"It's my turn to say I don't know," Beth said sadly. She sat up straighter. "You say you're leaving. Where will you go?"

"Where I was at first—doc's room back of his office. If I could get into that after dark, I could hide there."

Beth thought a moment, then nodded. "He always carries his black bag. He could bring your food in that."

Jim sighed. "I'm a damn nuisance to you, Beth. Once I get my head unscrambled, I'll get work and pay you and doc back. And maybe it'll come to me who I am."

"It'll happen. For sure."

"One more thing. After I'm gone, if anyone comes looking for me or old Hartman, let them in. Tell them they can search the house. Your story is this: you don't even know my name; I didn't say where I was going. And you're glad I'm gone because I couldn't pay you or doc."

Beth laughed softly and said, "I haven't lied since I was a little girl, but these lies I like."

5

It took all day and into the night for June to reach Mahaffy Station. By nightfall he knew he had a fever, but the bleeding had stopped under the neckerchief he had plastered on. He was in an agony he had never known. It was far more painful than the old wound covered by his beard had been. That had been a raking slash across his cheek by a gunsight; this had to be smashed bone and seemed to affect half his body.

When he rode into Mahaffy Station there was only one lamp lighted, and that was the night lamp in the ground-floor kitchen of the big log house. If the saloon was closed it meant it was late.

Now he lowered himself gently from the saddle to the ground and moved unsteadily toward the door which was never locked. He opened it, tripped over the sill, and his left hand slipped off the latch. He fell inside the room onto his injured shoulder and gave a great, agonizing, and uncontrollable shout of pain and fainted.

The first one to reach him was Norah, who ran from the bedroom, past the stairs, and into the kitchen. From upstairs there was a racket of footfalls on the floor and then the stairs.

Three men charged into the kitchen and halted at sight of the woman, still in her nightgown, kneeling beside June, whom she had turned over.

"Can you carry him into the bedroom? Be careful with him; he's shot in the shoulder." Norah rose

34

now, a full-figured woman with a rather worn face
that was beginning to erode. Going over to the stove,
she emptied the scuttle of coal into it and filled the
kettle. The three men were in their underwear, as un-
conscious of their undress as she was of her night-
dress. Passing them, she went into the bedroom,
lighted the lamp between the two beds and turned
down the covers of the unused bed.

Carefully, the three men carried him and laid him
on the bed. Norah found her wrapper and put it on,
then hunted through a dresser drawer and came up
with a pair of scissors. While the three men looked
on, she cut away June's bloody shirt and neckerchief,
and regarded the torn and bleeding flesh of June's
shoulder.

She said then, "Bring down some of your whiskey,
Jud. I'll clean him up."

June slept through the day and the next night,
interrupted by spells of delirium. The second morning,
he was rational and hungry. He was sitting up in
bed, his shoulder bandaged, when Norah came in to
collect his tray.

"Did I talk any nonsense when I was out of my
skull?"

"Nothing but," she answered calmly.

"Then forget it. Send the boys in when they're done
eating."

A few minutes later, three men, toothpicks in their
mouths, came in and closed the door behind them.
They had bid him good morning earlier; now two of
them, dirty and unshaven, seated themselves on
Norah's bed. The third, Jud Phillips, was taller, big-
ger, and cleaner than the others. He swung a straight-
back chair from the wall, straddled it, folded his arms
on its back, and regarded June with a hooded curiosity
in his amber cat's eyes, waiting.

One of the men on the bed, known as Benny Duplessis, cleared his throat preparatory to speaking.

June, scratching his beard with his good hand, anticipated him. "Boys, we're all in trouble, me the most. Now listen careful."

June began with the letter from Dock. Jud nodded in silence. He remembered Dock before he'd gone straight or partly straight. June told them of waiting and drygulching this marshal whose name was Tim Sefton. He'd thought he'd finished the job until Gus, the stage-driver, had told him of the man who'd been brought into the hospital with a cracked head and a total loss of memory. June then told wryly of his second attempt to drygulch Sefton, which had only earned him a bullet in the shoulder.

June finished by saying, "We got to get him before he gets us, before he remembers who the hell he is and where he was goin' and what for."

Jud spoke immediately. "You think he knew you from the bushwhack?"

"I'm dead sure he didn't. He had a gun stashed under his pillow. You would've too if you couldn't remember who it was shot you. You'd suspicion every stranger."

"You want us to try the same thing you did?" Jud asked skeptically.

"Yeah, but with a difference. You'll be wearing a marshal's badge—his."

Jud hesitated. "He'll know it's his."

"How? His name ain't on it. Reach behind you in that lowest drawer. The badge is in the back corner."

Jud half-rose, opened the lower drawer, found the badge, and examined it. It was star-shaped with only the legend "Dep. U.S. Marshal" engraved on it. "All right. What's my story?"

"You were sent up from the south to meet Tim Sefton in Driscoll. You weren't told why. The sheriff told you a shot man had been brought in to the hospital. No memory. You thought it might be him."

"Has the sheriff seen him?"

"Hell, I don't know," June said impatiently. "There's only two women there to fool—a Mex girl and the one that owns the house. You'll be in and out in five minutes."

"I don't know," Jud said dubiously, slowly.

"I do," June countered flatly. He looked at each of the three in turn. "Between all of you you're worth close to seven thousand dollars dead or alive to a lawman. Or me. I've had over eight months to turn you in. I didn't and I won't. All I want from you is protection. That's what you want too, ain't it?"

"What you want me and Joe to do?" Benny asked.

"Stay right here until Jud gets back. Watch the place for strangers." Now he looked at Jud. "Well, *hombre*, that's it. Take it or leave this place. It's up to you."

"I'll take it," Jud said with sudden decision.

June nodded with no surprise. "You ever shave a man, Jud?"

The swift change of subject held Jud speechless for a moment. Then he said, "Only me. Why?"

"Get Norah in here. I want her to cut my beard off and I want you to shave me because I can't do it myself."

Jud regarded him in silence, then smiled crookedly. "You think I'll miss Sefton, don't you? You think he'll come up here."

"Hell, I missed him twice. You might miss, too. I want him to be looking for a man with a beard. I'll take it from there."

"No you won't," Jud replied. "I'll bring back his ears."

6

It wasn't the same with Jim out of the house, Beth decided. She was sitting in her living room, the easy chair pulled over by the window to provide better light for the darning she was doing. Occasionally, she would look toward the sofa. It was as if she was expecting to see him sitting there where he had sat so many hours answering her questions with the same "I don't know, Beth."

She wondered now for the thousandth time what would happen to him. His dizziness and double vision had improved in the last two days, Dr. Rob had reported, but the past still remained a blank. The lonely hours he had twice spent in the room behind the doctor's office trying to remember something—anything— from his past were unavailing. Most certainly, Beth thought, when he was well enough to leave he should do so. Away from Driscoll, he wouldn't be shot at, but with no remembered skills he was fit for only the meanest labor.

She was yanked from her reverie by the sound of footsteps on the front porch. When a knock came on the front door, she knew it wasn't the doctor. She rose, put her mending basket aside, moved to the door, and opened it.

A tall clean-shaven man in his mid-thirties took off his hat, said, "Mornin', miss. I'm lookin' for the hospital, but this sure don't look like it to me."

Only then did Beth see the star pinned to his shirt. As he had lowered his hat from his long blond hair,

38

the edge of his worn duck jacket had been caught by the badge.

"But it is a hospital in the back rooms," Beth said. "Are you looking for someone?"

"Then I reckon you're Miss Avery. I'm Marshal Phillips from over in Silver City. Pleasure to meet you, miss."

Jim said to let anybody in, Beth thought. She swung the door wider and said, "Won't you come in?"

Phillips stepped past her and looked around the room, then watched her take off her apron and toss it on the sofa. She asked then, "Who is it you're looking for?"

"Let me ask you this first," Phillips said. "Was a man brought in here a week or so ago? He'd been shot in the head—big fellow, around thirty, near-red hair, green eyes, your sheriff said."

"Yes. He's been and gone. Just where, I don't know or care. He wasn't the best patient."

"Like how?"

"Cranky, didn't like the food, couldn't keep his hands off my hired girl, no money to pay. I wish I'd never seen him, even if I am sorry for him."

"Why sorry?"

"Yes. He doesn't know his own name. He can't remember who he is or where he came from or why he was here."

"So the sheriff said. Are you so sorry for him you're hiding him from me?"

"No, but perhaps I should. Three days ago a man came in to see another patient. He shot at the man we're talking about." Beth's tone of voice held an unmistakable chill. "I'll show you every room and closet in the house. Also the shed, if you'll follow me."

She began with the room where Hartman was sleeping, then led the silent Phillips upstairs. She opened every door of every room and closet and let him look. She even showed him Cruz's room in the attic. Fi-

nally, again downstairs, she knocked on the door of
Pearl's room, was bidden to enter, and showed him
that and its closet. Afterward, he went past Cruz,
who was washing clothes on the back porch and
looked through the shed. If her life depended on it,
she couldn't tell if this Phillips was a true marshal
or was posing as one.

Back in the living room, she faced him again. "Are
you satisfied now?"

Phillips's amber cat's eyes regarded her thoughtfully before he said, "I'm satisfied he ain't here, but I
ain't satisfied you don't know where he is."

A touch of fear came to her. She hoped it didn't
show in her face as she shook her head. "I can't tell
you something I don't know, can I?"

"Maybe you do know. Maybe you'll tell me after
I tell you this: your man is a deputy marshal, like me.
His name is Tim Sefton. We was to meet here
this week to work on a job together. I don't know
what job and neither did my boss. Sefton's boss
wanted a man that knew this country. I do. Sefton
would tell me what the job was." He shrugged. "If I
don't see him I likely go back and get fired. That's
why I got to see him."

Beth could not stop the wild beating of her heart.
Jim Battles was Deputy Marshal Tim Sefton. The
smile on her face now was not for Phillips, although it
must have seemed so to him. "I wish I could help you,
marshal, but I truly can't. He left without paying and
gave us a surly good-bye." She paused and looked
thoughtful. "He'd have had to get work to earn stage
fare. Why don't you ask around?"

"I'll do that," Phillips said, defeat in his tone of
voice.

"I hope you find him and don't lose your job."

"Me too," Phillips said. He let himself out and Beth
moved to the window to watch him ride out.

She sank down on the sofa, her heart still racing.

What was she to believe? That Phillips was a deputy
marshal she had no doubt, else how could he be
wearing the badge? How else would he know Tim
Sefton's name? "Sefton," she said aloud. It was a different, but nice-sounding name when spoken.

Back to Phillips again, she thought. He'd been ter-
ribly concerned about missing Tim—Jim. Was Phillips to work with him? Or arrest him? Jim had admitted to a feeling of guilt. Why?

She stood up now, wildly impatient to see and talk
with Jim. Yet a deep sense of caution warned against
it. If Phillips was watching her house, all he had to
do was follow her to his quarry. Best to take no
chances until after dark, and then Dr. Rob could es-
cort her.

Cruz was in the kitchen preparing dinner. When
Beth came in, Cruz said, "That man lookin' for Señor
Jim?" At Beth's nod, Cruz smiled as to a fellow con-
spirator. "Let him look."

A sudden thought came to Beth as she nodded.
She went over to the door of Pearl's room, heard the
invitation to enter, and went inside. Pearl was in her
wrapper, seated in an easy chair by the window, her
heavily bandaged foot resting on the only other chair
in the room, which was blue with cigarette smoke.

Beth closed the door and sat down at the foot of
Pearl's bed, where Pearl's crutches were leaned. As
Pearl stubbed out her cigarette in the saucer on her
lap, she asked, "Who was the snoop? Another one
lookin' for your fella'?"

Beth nodded, knowing she was blushing and not
caring. She said, "You looked at him as if you'd seen
him before."

"Maybe I have."

"Do you know his name?"

Pearl's sullen face still remained sullen in spite of her
short, gruff laugh. "Honey, in my business you don't
ask a man's name. You want him to know yours, so

he'll ask for you again, but he don't want you to know
his."

"Has he been to Widow Beaman's?"

"No."

"Then where did you remember him from?"

Pearl's glance fell away. She took a sack of tobacco
dust from her lap, took out a paper, shook tobacco
into it, and rolled a cigarette. Before she lighted it,
with the cigarette in her hand, she looked again at
Beth. "Maybe you don't want to know, a little lady
like you. Maybe I should tell doc and not you."

Beth tried to assess her tone of voice and decided
it held a derisive amusement. She said then, "Remember, I'm a doctor's daughter. I read his medical
books and what I didn't understand he'd tell me. If
you can say it, I can listen to it. I want to know about
this man."

Pearl struck a match on the floor, lighted her cigarette, and exhaled the smoke as she talked. "All right.
I used to work in a house in Corbett, over the mountains. He'd pay me and another girl to do things to
each other, so he could watch us. Sometimes he'd
even pay for other fellows to watch. My fella' didn't
like it, so he brought me over here."

"You're sure it's the same man?" Beth asked evenly.

"Sure I'm sure. You don't forget a crazy yellow-
eyes like that."

"When was it you left?"

"Well, I been here six-seven months."

"So he'd have to live within a day's ride from Corbett?"

"There's no sayin', is there? He come once a week,
sometimes twice. Reckon he lived fairly close."

Beth sat motionless, thinking. Silver City was over a
hundred miles to the west. If Phillips had lied about
where he worked, he probably lied about being a
marshal. Or, in the six or seven months since Pearl

had seen him, maybe he'd moved away and got a new job. She just couldn't know.

She sighed and rose. "Thanks, Pearl," and went out, closing the door against the smoke-drenched room.

"Shall I tell him right off we think we know his name, Rob?" Beth asked.

They were approaching Dr. Hasketh's small Main Street office. The early night sounds came from the saloons across the street and from the jingling of bits of the horses at the tie rails in front of them.

Dr. Hasketh thought a moment, then said, "Why don't you tell it to him the way you told it to me. Start with the knock on the door."

"Oh, I hope, I hope," Beth prayed softly.

The doctor unlocked the door of his office, stepped aside for Beth to enter, then went in and locked the door behind him. Inside, the night lamp was brighter than it appeared from the street through the frosted-glass window.

The doctor skirted his desk and glass-doored medicine cabinet. He moved through the room, Beth following. Halting before the door in the back wall, he knocked and said, "It's Beth and me, Jim."

The lock turned immediately and Beth preceded the doctor into the small room. Jim stood there, holding the doorknob and smiling. He looked approvingly at Beth's trim black wool suit and then grinned at the doctor. "Well, this beats talkin' to myself. Is there still a world out there?"

"A chilly one," Beth said. She gave a mock shiver and looked about the room. Nothing had changed since she was a girl: an operating table against the back wall, a blanket-covered cot to the left of the door, a nightstand between two chairs, and two heavily curtained small windows at rear and right.

The doctor put down his black bag full of the next

day's food for Jim and waited for Beth to take the
other chair. Jim said, "Take the cot, Beth. It's softer."

"No, we both want to watch your face when you
hear our news. You take it."

Jim looked quizzically from one to the other. "Something happening out there?" At Beth's nod, he moved
over to the cot, waited for Beth to seat herself, then
sat on the cot. Since he had not shaved for ten days
the dark beard stubble had further blurred the sharp
angles of his face that Beth remembered, but the
alertness and affection in his green eyes had not
dimmed. He was waiting for her to start.

"This morning I was sewing in the living room
when I heard a knock on the front door," she began.
She described Phillips with his tawny yellow eyes,
giving his name and not forgetting to mention he
wore a Deputy U.S. Marshal's badge on his shirt under
his jacket. Jim frowned in puzzlement at this. Was
there a look of apprehension in Jim's eyes, Beth wondered?

She went on to say Phillips had given her an exact
description of Jim, gotten from the sheriff. Beth had
told him his man, surly and broke, had left. When
Phillips suggested she was hidiing him, she took him
over every room and closet in the house, including
Pearl's. He even examined the shed. Afterward, back
in the house, he'd made one final plea. He was sent
out of Silver City to join another deputy marshal
coming down from the north; they would work together on the same job.

"He even gave me the name of the marshal he was
to join." She paused, isolating this. "The marshal's
name was Tim Sefton."

Jim came instantly to his feet, lips parted. "That's
me! That's my name! Tim Sefton!"

Beth rose; he held out his arms and she came to
him. He hugged her, lifted her off her feet, and swung

her in a circle and was laughing when he put her
down and released her.

Dr. Rob was laughing, too. "Welcome back to
reality, Tim."

Tim lifted Beth out of his way and twice paced
the short length of the room, then turned and halted.
"The marshal part's true. Deputy. I'm from Colorado." He frowned. "The town. It's gone, but I'll get
it."

"It'll come," the doctor said. "Everything will. But
sit down again, Tim. There's more."

Tim came back and sat down again, smiling at both.
Dr. Rob leaned his elbows on his knees, hands relaxed between his long legs. "Now I'll go slow. Take
your time answering, but don't worry if it's slow. All
right. How did you get down here?"

"That's pretty simple, Rob," Tim said. "There's no
train to here. Not by stage, because there would've
been a report of a stage robbery, and I was cleaned
out. So I must have come by horse. Maybe I had a
packhorse, too."

"Remember what you had on you? Some money,
of course, but what else?"

Tim frowned. "This isn't exactly remembering, Rob.
It's just what any deputy marshal would have on him.
Identification—a blanket letter from his boss to all
law officers asking their help."

"Would you have been wearing a badge?" Rob
asked.

Tim shook his head. "Not likely." At Rob's look of
disbelief, he added, "Oh I'd have it on me, but I
wouldn't be showing it. People will help you if they
think you're like them. They see a badge, they don't
know anything, because they don't want trouble."

Dr. Rob looked at Beth, then back to Tim. "I think
the star Phillips was wearing is yours, Tim."

"Then why didn't the man with the beard wear it?"
Tim asked.

"He didn't need to. He could get in by asking to see old Hartman. Phillips's try for you needed a better story to get at you. Phillips had the story and the star and your name."

"Bless him anyway," Tim said. "And bless you, Beth, for your lies to him." He added soberly, "So now there are two of them."

"Tell him what Pearl told you," Rob suggested.

Beth gave her account of her talk with Pearl after Phillips had left. It was factual, so much so that Tim wondered at her refusal to condemn Pearl's tawdry way of life. Beth finished by asking, "Doesn't that make it that Phillips lives within fairly easy riding distance from Corbett? And the man with the beard, too?"

There was a silence and then Dr. Rob asked, "Any memory of your assigned job, Tim?"

"No memory, just a hunch. If Phillips is hanging around Corbett then he must know the Beard. Since the Beard likely shot me first, then tried again, then sicked Phillips on me wearing my badge, it points to Corbett." He shrugged. "But the name means nothing to me. Where's Corbett?"

"The county seat of Mineral County, west over the Ramparts," Beth said.

"How'd they know I was coming?"

Dr. Rob said, "Did you ask any directions on the way?"

"I must have. The country was new, but if I asked it was only from lawmen, like I was taught."

"Who taught you?" Beth asked quietly.

Tim was silent in thought, then said, "I don't remember—yet." He gave them both a tired smile.

Dr. Rob stood up. "You've had enough for today, Tim. We'll see you tomorrow." They said good night to him and Dr. Rob let Beth and himself out onto the dark street.

Heading for home, Beth wasn't silent for long. "You think his memory will come back entirely?"

"Who knows?" the doctor said. Then added, "If it does, God help the Beard and Phillips."

Next morning when Dr. Rob came into his office, Tim was pacing the small confines of his room. After their greeting, Tim said, "Did some thinking after you left. This morning, too. You reckon you could take off this bandage for good?"

"Let's take a look." While Tim sat on the cot Dr. Rob cut away the bandage and looked at the wound. The stitches had healed nicely in the scar where the hair had been cut away. "I'll leave it off. When you comb your hair across it, it'll never show."

"I can go out on the street, then?"

"You've got something in mind?"

"A lot of things. Without that bandage and with a hat on and with this half-grown beard, I'm just another man." He hesitated. "How'd you get your specs, Rob?"

"Get them? Why, just like everybody else. I went to the store and tried 'em all on. I bought the pair I saw through best. Why?"

"Do they make them with just plain glass?"

"You mean with no magnification?" At Tim's nod, Rob grinned. "I can't tell you for sure, Tim, but I think so. I think a lot of preachers and schoolteachers and bankers figure specs make them look studious and wise, maybe. Doctors, too, but not this one. The damned things are a curse, but they're a blessing too if they let you see plainer and farther." He looked shrewdly at Tim. "I never heard of them curing double vision, though, if that's what you're wondering."

Tim actually laughed, as he had last night. He said, "No. It's not that. I'm going to Corbett on the morning stage tomorrow, now you say I can move. Trouble is, at least two men in Corbett know what I look like, but I'm not sure what they look like."

"So the specs are a disguise."

Tim nodded. "With some more of your clothes and some specs, I'm a buyer for a commission house in Kansas. Roundup's not far off and I want to beat the competition."

"Know anything about it?"

"I think I do, so I must. Anyway, it'll be all talk and an excuse for my being there."

"You'll need money."

Tim sighed. "Yes, but not much."

"Well, Beth thought of that; I'm meeting her at the bank later in the morning. Her house is clear and she'll get a loan."

"No, Rob—"

"Now don't get cussed with friends. You're still a deputy marshal on salary. Pay the loan off when you can." The doctor pulled a watch from his pocket, saw the time. He reached in his pocket, pulled out an eagle, and extended it to Tim. "That's for the glasses at Silberman's. Now give me a head start. We shouldn't be seen together."

7

At seven o'clock next morning, a tall bespectacled and bearded man, wearing a cotton duster over his clean duck jacket, entered the feed stable. He put down his valise, took money from his pocket, and paid the stable owner the stage fare to Corbett.

Afterward, he joined two other passengers who, valises on the ground beside them, were watching the teams being hitched up. The two appeared to Tim to be drummers of some sort, wearing townsmen's suits and hats. To them, Tim seemed a cross between a cowman and some sort of professional man, a lawyer maybe.

One of the hostlers came for their valises and deposited them in the rear boot, then opened the stage's door. The two drummers took the seat with its back to the driver, since it was better protected from dust and the weather. Tim took the rear seat, glad to be alone. Gus, the stage-driver, a canvas sack tucked in an armpit while pulling on his gauntlets, was last aboard. Once in the box he accepted the reins; he cursed the team into motion and the stage headed down Main Street.

As they pulled past Dr. Rob's office, Tim recalled their meeting last night. Beth had trimmed his hair. Dr. Rob had removed the scalp stitches, and he himself had trimmed his beard. Afterward, in the dark, they went back to Beth's place and ransacked Dr. Rob's wardrobe. The duck jacket, the duster, and the ancient Stetson were his, as was the valise. The hun-

49

dred dollars was in the money belt Dr. Rob had loaned him, as was the hip holster containing Dr. Avery's gun.

The steel-rimmed spectacles had set them all laughing. They and the beard added ten years to his age and gave him a completely false appearance of solemnity and, perhaps, wisdom. If the Beard over in Corbett took only five seconds to recognize him that was time enough.

As the stage climbed into the immediate foothills, Tim couldn't help but wonder what was ahead for him. He couldn't even guess and didn't try. He watched the piñon and juniper give way to pine and listened to the driver's whip and curses and felt the chill of the high country coming on.

It was close to noon when the first flakes of snow began to fall and melt. Watching them Tim suddenly thought: *Fort Lewis.* That was one more memory pulled out of the past.

An hour later, amidst the heavy-falling snowflakes, the stage pulled into a big clearing that held buildings and barns and corrals that loomed indistinctly through the banners of driven snow. The stage hauled up beside a big pole corral. Tim felt the stage rock and then the left door was opened by the stage-driver.

"Team change, gents," he announced. "There's whiskey across the street. It'll get colder ahead, I'm warnin' you."

Tim was out first. The two drummers piled out after him and, holding their hats on against the wind, trotted toward the store. Tim looked around at the buildings, then fell in beside the lanky stage-driver, who was grasping the same canvas sack he had been holding before. This time, Tim could see the stenciled letters U.S. MAIL on the side of the sack.

"You the postmaster, too?" Tim asked.

"No, but the only way they get it is by me."

They mounted the steps together and were immediately out of the wind and snow. Tim wanted to ask something else, but the driver went through the door. Tim's new spectacles were blurred with snow water so that he could barely see the door. He went inside, halted immediately, and wondered if he would have to let the glasses dry. Then he remembered seeing old codgers wiping spectacles clean with their shirttails or neckerchief or handkerchief. His neckerchief was clean and he used it to carefully wipe his glasses. Once he could see through them again, he headed for the sound of voices and found himself in a small saloon whose bar was tended by an old man wearing black sleeve cuffs over his wrists.

Besides the two drummers at the bar there were two cowhands playing rummy at one of the card tables. They observed his entrance and went on playing. Tim came up beside the stage-driver who already had a glass of whiskey before him. He was answering a question: "Oh, him. He cleared out three-four days ago."

Tim ordered whiskey and was given a glass and bottle by the old man, who now picked up the mail sack, rounded the end of the bar, and left the room with the sack.

Tim poured his drink, tasted it, and then remembered what it was he wanted to ask the stage-driver. He said, "Supposing I wanted to send a letter to someone here. How would I address it?"

"Why, Driscoll, Mahaffy Station. This here is it. Or Corbett, Mahaffy Station. Either way, I'd deliver the letter."

When Tim heard Mahaffy Station it registered with a swiftness that was stunning. *This is it!* Memory shouted so strongly he wondered if he'd spoken aloud. *This is where I was heading!*

His hand was shaking as he raised his glass. The

driver was filling his own glass and did not notice. With the glass safely on the counter again, Tim asked idly, "Is that old boy Mahaffy?"

"No. He just works here. Mahaffy's dead."

"Then who owns this?"

"Fella named June Constable."

Again, Tim felt a wild exultation. He remembered the name! And what he could now associate with that name warned him. *No more questions.*

One of the drummers asked for the bottle and Tim passed it on to him. Slowly, but certainly, memory was returning, he realized.

Then the stage-driver announced the next drink would be the last. Tim sloshed some whiskey in his glass. The old man returned with the mail sack. Tim finished his drink, paid up, and went out on the porch. The snow flurry had passed momentarily and he could see Mahaffy Station in its sorry entirety.

Assuming each shack held a couple of people and the big house a dozen, the whole settlement wouldn't account for more than thirty people. A stranger only riding through would be noticed. A stranger staying just one night would draw instant attention and curiosity. A longer stay would invite suspicion, surveillance and, inevitably, a bushwhack. Staying here any length of time would be like living in a store window with no excuse for being there.

The driver and the drummers came out and Tim followed them across the road. Before he climbed up to the box the driver said, "There's buffalo robes under that center seat."

As they headed out for the climb to the pass, Tim put his returning memory to the test. The marshal up north—Barry by name, he now recalled—had asked for the loan of him from Fort Lewis. His own deputies were too well known; any move by them would flush this wild bunch out of the country.

The gang was very small and very expert and none

of them had a record of arrests. Neither had they ever been photographed. Those were June's unbreakable laws. When a job called for more men than they had, June would recruit outside help, with this proviso: once the job was pulled off, they would meet at a designated spot and split the loot, but the temporary recruits would have to stay away from Mahaffy Station. If they were seen there, they'd be gunned down. His own small group would split up and separately return to the station. The money split on any job was half to June and his small band, half to the temporary recruits.

How had Barry come upon this information? He'd arrested one of June's temporary recruits for murder. In exchange for a lesser charge, he had told how June operated and where.

There was something else Barry had told him, but for the moment Tim couldn't remember what. It was truly snowing now and he reached down for a buffalo robe. The two drummers were already sharing one.

They were on the west slope of the Ramparts and Tim was still playing his game of remembering. Then, as if unbidden, he recalled what else Barry had told him. It was that the sheriff of Mineral County couldn't help but know of this odd crew at Mahaffy Station and their strange comings and goings. Since Barry had never had any inquiries on these men from the sheriff, it stood to reason he was being paid to ignore them. Don't trust Sheriff Ben Clay, Barry had said.

Tim smiled now, asking silently, *How's that for remembering, Beth and Rob?*

The stage reached Corbett after dark. Tim had lost track of what day in the week it was, but by the time the stage reached the center of town he was sure it was Saturday night. A church they'd passed had been lighted up, with buggies lined up before it for some sort of church social.

In the business district some of the stores were still

open. The saloons were doing a booming business, especially the one across from the biggest hotel in front
of which the stage pulled up.

Tim retrieved his valise from the boot, climbed the
two steps to the hotel veranda, and went inside. The
desk was at the far end of the lobby. He was ahead
of the two drummers and registered under the name
of H. Simons. His room was five doors down the left
corridor. Without bothering to light the lamp in his
room, he peeled out of his duster, pitched it and his
valise in the chair, and went out.

As he had his supper in a café next to the hotel, he
pondered his next move—or any move. A return to
Mahaffy Station was out. Bait June to come into Corbett? How? There was a railroad here, so there was a
telegraph. Should he wire Barry to send him the credentials stolen from him? Sheriff Ben Clay would
know of it in minutes, and send a message to June.
His identity as H. Simons would be gone. Besides,
what use were his credentials and a badge? Both
would only insure him of certain attack by June and
his crew. He didn't know. One thing he was sure of,
however, was that unless he intended to just sit here
in Corbett, he must have a horse. That, plus saddle
and blankets, would eat up most of his money. He
was, or had been, a better-than-fair poker player.
Why not try for some money that way?

Finished with supper, he headed across the street
for the big saloon, across whose white-painted false
front was painted in four-foot-high letters, THE
UNION. Shouldering through the batwings he was in
a big, smoky, and noisy room jammed with men. The
crowded bar was on the left; the rest of the room,
save for a narrow aisle for a passageway, held the
card tables, all seats occupied. The faro layout was
against the right wall, surrounded by players, the
watcher in a tall chair with a shotgun resting on the
chair arms. Men were watching some of the games,

drinks in hand. The noise, of course, came from the men at the bar, and now Tim walked three quarters of its length before he found a space at it.

A slim, tired-looking bartender appeared before him and said, "What'll it be, perfesser?"

Tim ordered a whiskey and smiled. His spectacles accounted for the professor greeting, he supposed. When he had paid for his drink, he faced the room, elbows on the bar, drink in hand, and watched. The game at the biggest table was being watched by a half-dozen men which indicated a high-stake game. Mild curiosity pushing him, Tim moved over to it.

There were six men in the game of stud. A new hand had just been dealt them. It was then that Tim noticed the star on the vest of a swarthy man with close-cropped gray hair. The pile of chips to his right was the biggest of the lot. Was this Sheriff Ben Clay? Tim wondered, and guessed it was. A deputy sheriff would be younger.

The betting was mild until it reached the sheriff; he bumped it. The next man turned his cards face down. The man past him raised, then looked at the sheriff, and grinned.

Tim's heart jumped.

This tall man had long pale hair under his tipped-back Stetson. He had amber cat's eyes, good teeth, a squarish jaw. *Beth's exact description of Phillips,* Tim thought. He watched him; when it was the turn of the man seated just below Tim to bet, Tim saw those amber cat's eyes square-on.

Tim finished his drink, went back to the bar, and signaled the same bartender. When the man put the bottle before him, Tim asked, "You know those men playing with the sheriff?"

A sudden blandness came into the bartender's expression. "Don't even have to look, perfesser. They got a game every Saturday night."

"The second fella on the left of the sheriff. He call himself Morgan?"

The bartender didn't even look. "Why don't you ask him?"

"Don't want to bust into the game is why. Is his name Morgan?"

Still the bartender didn't look. "Nobody named Morgan in that bunch," he said, and walked away into the din of the upper bar.

That ought to start something, Tim thought. He poured his drink, sampled it, and waited. Watching the back-bar mirror, he presently saw a heavyset cowpuncher come up to Phillips and say something to him. Phillips listened, looked over at the bar, and said something to the cowpuncher, who left immediately.

In less than a minute, Tim felt a tap on his left shoulder. He half-turned and saw the beefy cowpuncher facing him. The man appeared to be in his forties; he was dirty, his muddy eyes dulled with liquor, and his belly overlapped his belt under his vest. His gun was on his left hip, riding low.

"I hear you're lookin' for a Morgan. I'm Morgan. Wuddia want with me?"

"Nothing," Tim said, putting down his glass. "You're the wrong Morgan."

The puncher grinned, revealing rotten teeth. "Take another look, four eyes. Wipe your specs first."

Instantly Tim cuffed him with the flat of his left palm across the ear. It did what Tim intended; the thunderclap in his ear drove the puncher sideways, so that his left forearm was pinned under the overhang of the bar, canceling any possibility of a quick draw.

Tim's savage cross-blow was aimed at the very peak of the bloated belly. He heard the wind gust out of the man with an explosive, ragged roar. The force of it drove the puncher back-pedaling into the drinker

behind him, who caromed into two other unwary
drinkers. Taken off-balance, they lurched into their
neighbors. Drinks fell to the floor and there was wild
cursing, each man going for the one he thought
bumped him. Inevitably, one man was driven into a
gaming table, spilling chips and cards and bringing
on the fighting fury of the players who broke up a
second card game. The bartenders were kneeling on
the bar top, swinging sawed-off pool cues at anyone
they could hit. Other gamblers, seeing their games
and chips endangered, joined in trying to shove this
seething mass of men toward the door.

Tim, alone at the bar, took the gun from the big,
now-vomiting puncher who was on his hands and
knees, put it on the bar top, and finished his drink.

The sheriff finally fired two shots into the ceiling
and waded into the mob, yelling, "Take it outside!
Take it outside!" He was rapping skulls right and left
with his gun barrel, shoving and kicking men toward
the door.

A voice from behind Tim said now, "Take a closer look, mister. Am I your Morgan?"

Tim turned slowly to face Phillips. They were about
of a height, and there was tense wariness in Phillips's
face. Tim shook his head slowly and smiled. "Another
wrong Morgan. No, you're not him."

Phillips relaxed and grinned. "What made you think
I was? And who's Morgan?"

"Well, Morgan and me got into some trouble together. That was four-five years back. We had to split
up, and I haven't seen him since. He was wearin' a
beard then, so I didn't rightfully know what he looked
like. Still, he had your size and your color eyes, and
you don't see that often—the color, I mean."

"No," Phillips agreed.

The puncher had stopped retching and Phillips and
Tim watched him haul himself unsteadily to his feet.
Tim slid the bottle of whiskey down to him, picked

up his gun by its barrel, and handed it butt first to
Phillips, saying, "You better keep that till I'm out of
here."

Phillips laughed and rammed the gun in his belt.
The racket by the door had been moved out into the
street. The bartenders were surveying the wreckage
of broken chairs and scattered chips and lost hats.
Now the sheriff came through the door, holstering his
gun, and made directly for Tim. His swarthy face was
even darker now as he approached. He was bare-
headed, breathing hard, and still angry as he skirted
the puncher and hauled up before Tim.

"You started this," Sheriff Clay said flatly. "Why?"

Tim nodded toward the puncher. "Want to get his
story first?"

"No, I want yours first."

Tim told it as it happened. His guess, he said, was
that the bartender told the puncher to warn "this
man," indicating Phillips, that somebody was snoop-
ing.

Tim looked at Phillips and said, "I still don't know
your name, except it's not Morgan."

"He's Jud Phillips. Go on," the sheriff said impatiently.

Tim did so. When he finished, the sheriff gave a
glance of bewilderment to Phillips, then again settled
his attention on Tim.

"You're saying this started because Russ here—"
he indicated the puncher with a nod of his head—
"told you to wipe your specs?"

"You weren't listening," Tim said. "He said, 'Take
another look, four eyes.'"

Again the sheriff looked at Phillips. His anger was
giving way to unconcealed bafflement.

Tim, seeing this, touched his spectacles and said,
"I've worn these since I was seven. Every year of
school I had a dozen fights. Any kid called me four

eyes had a scrap on his hands. If I couldn't lick him the first time, I did the second."

"Why?"

Tim thought a moment. "All right. If you were born with a harelip and the kids called you bunny, what would you do? Say you were born with a hunchback and the kids called you humpy. Or with buck teeth and the kids called you horsy." He nodded to the puncher. "What if I'd answered his four eyes by calling him pasgut? I'd have bought a fight right there." He paused, watching the sheriff. "Any of that mean anything to you, nigger?"

For a moment, Tim thought he'd gone too far, and then the sheriff exploded into laughter. So did Phillips, and Tim smiled in relief.

"Yeah, I see what you mean." Now he looked back at one of the bartenders and the houseman cleaning up the wreckage. "Still, you're to blame for wrecking this place."

Phillips cut in, "Ah, the hell with it, Ben. I've seen it wrecked worse and so have you. It's payday, the boys got drunk, and wanted a little fun. Nobody's hurt, and the bar mirror ain't busted. Let it go."

The sheriff sighed. "I reckon you're right."

A couple of the bartenders were behind the bar again and a trickle of the less belligerent drinkers were coming in off the street. Tim beckoned a bartender who picked up glasses and a bottle and came down and put the makings on the bar.

When they had poured their drinks and Tim had paid for them, he said, "Funny thing. What started this ruckus was me asking the bartender if you were Morgan." At Phillips's nod he continued, "I really am lookin' for a Morgan." His glance shifted to the sheriff. "Know any Morgan around here, sheriff?"

"What's his front name?"

"Lee. About my age and size."

The sheriff thought a moment, then shook his

head. "I know two Morgans, brothers, but they're both old men." He finished his drink and said, "I'm cashin' in my chips, Jud. Then I'm goin' home to bed." He looked at Tim. "Who do I thank for the drink and the fireworks?"

"Name's Hal Simons, sheriff."

"Thanks, and see you around." He left for his poker table.

When he was gone, Tim observed, "Nice fella' for a lawman. And thanks for gettin' him off my back."

Phillips smiled faintly and nodded, then looked at Tim and said, "You know, you're a stubborn cuss. You want this Morgan bad—so bad you wreck a saloon over him and then ask the sheriff if he can help you find him."

"I just need him."

"For more trouble, like before?"

"It don't have to be," Tim said. He finished his drink, then said, "I'm short on sleep. I better go get some."

"Be around a spell?"

"Till the next stage East. No use hangin' around here."

"Well, good night, four eyes." He was smiling.

"Same to you, cat eyes," Tim replied, and he, too, was smiling.

Back in his room Tim noted the lamp was lighted, his bed turned down, and his valise and duster at the foot of his bed. There was also a faint smell of tobacco smoke. He was reasonably sure that one of Sheriff Clay's deputies had rousted out the housekeeper to have a look at his belongings, since the sheriff seemed a capable, careful man.

He dug a cigar out of his valise, pulled the lone easy chair up to the bed, pulled down the shade of the single window, lighted his cigar, sat down, and put his feet up on the bed.

Carefully, then, he began to review and assess what had happened tonight. There was no doubt in his mind that Jud Phillips was the phony marshal June Constable had sent to Beth's to kill him. Had Phillips tonight suspected his identity? He thought not, because Phillips would have reacted differently if he were suspicious; he would have slipped out of The Union, waited outside, braced him, questioned him, and gunned him down. Instead, Phillips had confronted him quietly.

The next question Tim put to himself was whether or not he had made his search for the nonexistent Morgan convincing. He thought he had. His asking after Morgan from the sheriff had been the clincher. Also, his guarded hints as to why he wanted to find Morgan had roused Phillips's curiosity. Proof of this was Phillips asking if he would be around long. That meant another talk with Phillips, almost surely.

Tim spent the next hour wondering how much and what to tell Phillips. When he had decided, he blew the lamp and went to bed. Before he slept, he thought of Beth and Doc. He had left them fearful of his safety and his memory, but there was no need to worry about the memory returning. When he'd signed the register downstairs he used the maiden name of his great-grandmother on his mother's side. That took pretty good remembering. . . .

Next morning, a bright and sunny fall day, Tim headed for breakfast at the same café. There were a half-dozen men seated at the big round family table —and one of them was Phillips. *So soon,* Tim thought with pleasure.

Jud waved him over and Tim took the chair beside him.

"Been to the Nightriders' Church?" Jud asked.

"Don't know where it is."

Jud grinned. "That's a local joke. It's where we

were last night. Sunday up till noon it's locked. The front door, that is. The back door is open for anyone with the shakes."

"With the preacher sayin' 'Go and Sin Some More,' eh?"

Jud laughed. "That's about it."

The fat waitress came up with platters of meat and potatoes and eggs and filled Tim's mug with coffee and refilled Jud's. Tim began to eat hungrily.

"About last night," Jud said. "What did you have in mind if you found Morgan?"

Without looking up, Tim said quietly, "Not here."

While Tim ate his breakfast they talked of the early snows which never lasted, the price of cattle, range prospects for the coming winter, and local politics—all subjects that allowed overhearing.

Finished, they both paid up and went out on the boardwalk. Jud looked across the street and asked, "The church all right?"

Tim nodded and they headed across the almost-empty street, taking the alley beside The Union, past the loading dock, and to the back door. It let on to a dark, short corridor through which Tim could see the barroom with several men standing at the bar.

Leading the way, Jud halted in the corridor, opened a door on the right, and looked in. He beckoned Tim, who came up and looked into the room. It was a private card room holding two large tables and chairs. By the light coming through the back and side windows Tim could see it had been swept and cleaned since last night. He nodded, and Jud said, "I was nightridin' last night for sure. I could use a drink. You?"

Again Tim nodded and moved into the room while Jud went on up the corridor. Tim pulled out a chair and sat down at the table. He was still reviewing how he hoped to handle this when Jud returned with two glasses of whiskey. Putting them on the table, he shut the door, then came over and seated himself, thumbed his Stetson off his forehead, picked up his drink, and took a long swallow. Afterward, he took out a sack of tobacco and began to roll a cigarette.

Tim said evenly, "You were wonderin' what I had in mind if I found Morgan." At Jud's nod, he added, "Well, keep wonderin'."

Jud looked up, a touch of temper in his yellow eyes. When he spoke, his voice was even. "Why? Ain't you been treated right?"

"Better than right. Maybe too right."

"Like how?"

Tim pretended to think a moment, then said, "All right. You're friends with Sheriff Clay. He does what you say. He did last night, didn't he?"

Jud lit his cigarette, inhaled, and nodded.

"If I tell you what I plan if I find Morgan, you can do two things. You can tell Clay to arrest me for last night and I'll be in jail out of your way. Then you can round up some friends and pull the job I've planned for a year. Make sense?"

"No. If you found it, you boss it."

"*You* say," Tim said with quiet sarcasm.

"I figured you needed help. You said so yourself!" Jud said hotly.

"I do. I'll say it again." He paused long enough to take a sip of his drink. "Just what the hell do I know about you except you're a nice-seemin' fella?"

"That's all I know about you, too," Jud countered. "Maybe you're nothin' but talk."

"No, I can prove I'm not." He rose and began to circle the other table, head down, thinking. Halting suddenly, he looked at Jud and asked, "How many men can I count on?"

"At least five, countin' me. More than that, but it'll take time."

"You their boss?"

"No. And unless I know what you know I won't even tell the boss I talked to you."

Tim resumed pacing. *I've been hard to get long enough,* he decided. He went back to his drink, downed half of it, then said, "Looks like we'll have to trust each other, don't it?"

"That's what I been tryin' to tell you," Jud said flatly.

Tim looked down at him. "The last time I said that it bought me two shots in the leg. Since then, I've been careful." Jud said nothing and Tim made another circle of the table.

He sat down in his chair. "Tell you what I'll do. How long'll it take to round up your boys?"

"Hell, they're close," Jud said. "It's the boss I'm worryin' about. You see, he's careful too."

"Fair enough. Now, how does this sound? I can't find Morgan and I wouldn't ask him in this if I could, now you might be in it. Know where Stone's Ferry is? North of Driscoll." At Jud's nod Tim went on, "I'm headin' for there tomorrow. I'll be there for three days. That give you enough time to talk to your boss?"

"Why there? It's only a store and a house."

"I hid out there once for a month. They rent rooms and feed you. The stage changes teams there, so we can pick up the northbound stage there."

"Me? What for?"

Tim's expression was one of surprise. He said patiently, "Why, to look over the layout, map the buildings, and road, watch the guard system, learn their habits and make careful notes about everything."

Jud was frowning, not liking this. Tim asked coldly, "Have you ever pulled off a job without scoutin' it first?"

"No, but if you been on this for a year, you know all there is to know."

"Don't try and pull that on me," Tim said flatly.

"I'll be with you and your boys when we move in. If anything goes wrong, guess who gets shot in the back. Me." He shook his head. "If you won't look it over first, then forget it. Your boss would tell you the same thing."

"All right, all right!" Jud said, half-angry. He was silent a moment, then finished his drink. "How big is this, you reckon?"

"Eighty thousand, give or take a little."

Jud's amber eyes came alert. "That's big, for sure."

"The split is fifty-fifty—half to me, half to you. I'll have some friends with me when we count it, too."

Jud nodded and stood up. "If I'm not there by Thursday, the boss don't like it."

Tim rose. "I take off after breakfast Thursday, with or without you. Tell your boss that."

8

Phillips and fat Russ reached Mahaffy Station just after midday. There were a couple of inches of melting snow on the ground, but the day was bright and sunny with a snow glare a man had to squint his eyes against.

They dismounted at the corral. Jud gave Russ his reins, then opened the gate, waited until both horses were through, and closed it. He headed straight across the muddy road for the big log house, wondering what June would make of what he was about to hear.

He went in without knocking and, unbuttoning his sheepskin, turned into the kitchen and found the usual card game about to begin.

"Got any money left, Jud, or did the girls get it all?" Benny called in greeting.

"They got it," Jud said cheerfully. He moved over to the table and said, "Why don't you fellas move the game over to the store? I got business with June."

They looked at June at the head of the table. He nodded and said, "Leave the bottle." Jud, looking at him, thought, *Jesus, he's ugly*, and looked away. The bearded June wasn't a bad-looking man, but now the livid six-inch scar on his left cheek looked as if it would bleed again any moment.

The cardplayers moved out. Jud shucked out of his sheepskin, threw it and his hat on the bench, then poured himself a drink into one of the clustered glasses on the table. He held it up, looked inquiringly at

June, who only shook his head, then took a deep drink.

Placing his glass on the table he said, "I've got the goddamnedest story you ever heard."

"Well, I've heard plenty of 'em. Let's hear yours."

Jud sat down on the bench and began his story with Russ passing on to him the bartender's warning a man was looking for a fellow named Morgan, and thought he was Morgan. Jud told him to go back and identify himself as Morgan. When Russ did just that, the stranger slugged him, starting a brawl that involved more than half the men in the saloon.

Here, June interrupted him. "Why did he think you were Morgan?"

"Color of my eyes."

"What's the color of his eyes?"

Jud hesitated, then said, "Blue or green. Couldn't rightly tell because he was wearin' specs."

"He fought Russ and never took off his specs?" June asked skeptically.

"He didn't have to fight him. He had Russ on the floor and pukin' with just two swipes."

June was about to speak, but didn't. He nodded and Jud took up his monologue again. The sheriff was pacified. The stranger, whose name was Hal Simons, even asked Sheriff Clay about Morgan and Clay couldn't tell him.

"Of course, he asked him," June said skeptically. "How could Ben know about a Morgan that ain't?"

"Maybe," Jud said. Then he told of his session with Simons this morning, how Simons refused flatly to tell him where the hit was to be made and what it was and why he wouldn't tell him. Then Jud made Simons's last point: either Jud or one of them must come with him from Stone's Ferry to look over the layout or the deal was off. He didn't want to get shot in the back if something went wrong.

"That's the way it stands now. If I'm not there by

Thursday mornin', he rides out. I told him if I didn't show it meant you didn't like it."

For some reason June didn't understand, he didn't like it. Was he resentful of Jud's turning this up, when he himself usually came up with the jobs? He didn't think so. A job was a job, no matter who thought it up.

But why hadn't Simons come straight to him? It could be he'd heard that anyone with a record was unwelcome here, so he'd played it safe by talking to Jud. That probably meant he had a record a yard long.

This Simons was pretty coony, everything considered. He'd refused to tell where the hit was to be made for fear of being beat to it. And he wanted it scouted by somebody besides himself. Both were signs of a careful man who'd been burned before.

Jud had been right, too, in pointing out it was time to get moving. If they couldn't turn up something soon, the boys would drift. He'd hate like hell to lose them, especially Jud, who was bright, tough and loyal, and a friend.

He finished his drink. It tasted sour.

9

Tim's stage got into Driscoll after dark. He had a quick meal of bacon and eggs at a café, but he was so impatient to see Beth and Rob that he passed up his pie and second cup of coffee, then paid and left.

As he walked toward Beth's house, it seemed to him he'd been gone a week. Approaching the house, he saw lamplight coming from the second-story window. A new roomer, maybe. Lamps were lighted on the ground floor and as he mounted the steps a notion came to him that made him smile. He knocked on the door, then fell back a step, and put his valise on the floor beside him.

Beth opened the door. Tim said in a gravelly voice, "You the lady that rents rooms, miss?"

Beth peered at him in the near-darkness. Making out the valise beside him, she said cautiously, "Why yes. Won't you come in?"

She swung the door wider, watching his lower body come into the lamplight, started to turn into the room, hesitated, then turned to face him as all of him was lamplit.

"Oh, Tim, you devil!"

She came into his open arms as if it had been planned. "Tim, Tim, how we've worried about you!" She pressed her body against his, stood on tiptoe, and they kissed. As they parted she took his hand, turned and called. "Dr. Rob! Hurry! Tim's back!"

Dr. Rob came out of the kitchen, ripping off the dishtowel tucked in his belt. He tossed it on the dining-room table as he passed and came into the living room, hand extended. As he and Tim shook hands, both were smiling.

Dr. Rob looked him over and said, "I take it the natives were friendly over there. I don't see any bandages."

"Not any," Tim said. Now he took off his spectacles and put them in his shirt pocket. "I've been waiting two days to ask you this. Can you remember your great-grandmother's maiden name on your mother's side?"

Dr. Rob looked puzzled, frowned at the effort to remember, then said, "No. If I ever knew it I've forgotten. Why?"

"I can remember mine's. It was Mattie Simons."

Only then did Dr. Rob comprehend what Tim was telling him. "It's come back, hasn't it! All the way?"

"All I ever had."

Dr. Rob was smiling. "That," he said, "calls for one helluva big drink. Talk to Beth about anything, but where you've been and what happened until I get back." He turned and headed for the kitchen. Beth and Tim, hand in hand, moved to the sofa and sat down.

"There's a new light upstairs. New roomer?"

Beth shook her head. "No. I was sewing up there. I wish it was a roomer. I think this big house scares people off. Or I do."

"It didn't scare Rob off and you didn't scare Rob off."

When Dr. Rob came in with the drinks, he handed them around, then proposed a ceremonial toast "to friends assembled." They drank to that, and Dr. Rob pulled up an easy chair to face them. He sat down and said to Tim. "Start where you want, Tim."

Tim began with his discovery that Mahaffy Station was his assignment. He told it all—guesses, judgments, hopes, and his reasons for them.

Finished, they were all silent. Dr. Rob finally broke it. "What's your guess, Tim. Will Phillips meet you at Stone's Ferry?"

"If it was up to him alone, I think he would. June's something else."

Beth asked, "But if he does come what do you show him? You've already said you made up your story out of whole cloth."

"There are a half-dozen big mines up north. Big banks, too, to handle payrolls. Say I pick out The First National of Galena for our hit."

"All mines don't pay off on the same day, I've heard," Dr. Rob said. "That's because the banks don't want that much money on hand."

"That's only my story to him. We'll reach Galena together, and I'll hand him over to Marshal Barry."

Dr. Rob frowned. "On what charges?"

"I'll be in Stone's Ferry by noon Wednesday. If Phillips is there that night, we talk about this new job. I'll recollect some old ones. He will, too, because we're working together. I'll have a dozen charges ready for Barry."

"If you say so," Dr. Rob said. He took a sip of his drink, wiped his mouth with the back of his hand, and said, "That'll be one gone. But you want June Constable and his whole bunch. That means you'll have to go back time after time to Mahaffy Station, each time with a new story. With Phillips in jail, wouldn't you reckon on your next trip they'd swarm all over you?"

"I'll think of something," Tim said easily.

Beth exchanged glances with Dr. Rob, who shrugged slightly. Beth looked at Tim and shook her head. "This doesn't sound like you, not the Tim that left here."

"I'm not that Tim. All the time here, I was a scared cripple. I'm not any more," Tim said.

Beth persisted, though. "You said you'll think of

something. Think of it now. The thought of you going back to Mahaffy Station again and again gives
me the shivers. It gives Dr. Rob the shivers, too,
though he probably won't admit it. How do you go
back?"

Tim reached out and squeezed her hand. "I don't
know, Beth. Did I know what I was going to do when
I spotted Phillips in that Corbett saloon? No, but I'm
here."

Beth sighed. "I like to plan my life, to know what
I'll do ahead of time. You lied your way out of Corbett, and you'll be lying your way into Galena. You'll
lie your way back into Mahaffy Station." She withdrew
her hand. "It's no way to live, Tim. You'll get killed
in a lie, and that's no way to die, damn it!"

"No," Tim agreed.

Tuesday was a strange, uncomfortable day, and it
shouldn't have been. Tim'd slept late in one of the
middle bedrooms upstairs, and when he went below
both Cruz and Beth served him breakfast in the kitch-
en. Pearl, whom he'd never seen, was in her bedroom,
door closed. Dr. Rob was at his office.

Beth, having coffee across the kitchen table while
he ate, was cheerful enough, but there was something
different about her. Twice he surprised her watching
him, almost studying him. Her gray eyes were sad,
even when she smiled. It was as if she was waiting
for him to tell her something, to go beyond last
night's talk, to somehow reassure her. And he couldn't.

He raked Beth's yard and burned the leaves. He
went shopping with Beth. He walked around town.

Supper and afterward was better. Dr. Rob and
Beth good-naturedly challenged the full return of his
memory. He found himself talking about growing up
on a Colorado ranch. He'd got all the schooling he
could afford, then read for the law in the offices of a
district attorney. He'd haunted courtrooms, learning

the law, working as a night marshal to earn a living. Inevitably, he came in contact with U.S. Marshals. Finally, the commissioner, valuing his law background, recruited him as a Deputy U.S. Marshal. He guessed he'd done a good job because the commissioner had chosen him to come down and help Barry nail June and his bunch.

Beth asked the questions about his family and boyhood; it was as if she was searching for something to explain his foolhardy recklessness in Corbett. Dr. Rob was more interested in hearing details of how he had carried out past assignments, as if they might confirm his feeling that Tim, if the situation demanded, could draw on an instant cunning and deviousness, like a wise and wary animal.

When they parted for bed, Tim had the feeling he had been sat upon in judgment and had not come off very well.

Next morning Tim left the house early, before anyone was up. He'd said his good-byes last night, with thanks and a promise he'd keep in touch.

By the time he'd had a quick breakfast and crossed the street to the feed stable the stage teams were being driven out of the corral, the passengers already settled in the coach. As he took his seat he saw that Jud Phillips was not one of the passengers. Had he chosen to ride over to Stone's Ferry or had June vetoed the plan?

It was close to noon when the stage slowed on the near shore of the Clearwater River. Across the slow-flowing water, Tim could see the cottonwood motte which almost hid Stone's store and the big frame house beyond it. He had stayed there on the ride down.

The ferry was simply a big-railed scow capable of taking the stage and its team: it was nosed against the shore now with its plank ramp down. As soon as the stage was loaded, the ferryman raised the ramp and poled the scow out into the current. The cable anchored to the far shore ran through two big iron rings ironed to the scow side. The scow was headed across and downstream, the river's current propelling it.

On the bank, the front ramp was lowered and the stage driven off. A waiting team on the shore was ready to tow the scow and cable upriver for the crossing back.

The stage slowed at the store in preparation for its stop at the house beyond. But Tim had seen what he wanted. Jud Phillips sat scowling in one of the porch chairs in the shade of the veranda roof.

The stage-driver called down, "Half hour for dinner, folks."

Tim climbed out of the stage and saw Jud Phillips approaching, but pretended not to. He was retrieving his valise from the boot when a surly voice said behind him. "Where the hell you been, Simons? We've shot a day already."

Tim turned slowly and surveyed Jud without smiling. "I said I was leavin' Thursday mornin', and so I will."

"Maybe you will. Maybe I'll leave before that."

"Suit yourself," Tim said quietly.

"Ah, why we hackin' at each other? Come on and have a drink."

"Where?"

"I got a bottle in my room."

They trailed the other stage passengers into a front room that had been converted into a dining room holding two trestle tables and benches. The stair to the second floor was on the far wall. On his way to it, Jud picked up a glass from one of the table settings and led the way up the stairs to his room that held two metal cots, a washstand, and a straight-back chair beside each cot.

Jud put the glass on the washstand beside another one, reached for the bottle of whiskey under his bed, then poured a half glass of whiskey into each glass.

Tim accepted his and watered it from the pitcher on the washstand under Jud's amused surveillance. He raised his glass and said, "Here's to us—three, four, five, six. How many?"

"We'll see. It all depends on what you got in mind."

"The less you are, the richer you'll be, but not too few," Tim said. They both drank, then sat down on their cots, facing each other, glasses in hand.

Jud said, after a scowling silence, "Well, I'm here. Where do we go and what do we do?"

"That'll come later."

"Why not now—*right* now?" Jud asked. His gun was suddenly in his hand in one effortless motion.

"Listen careful, will you?" Tim said wearily. "There were four other men on that stage with me. How do I know they're not your bunch? If I tell you what you just asked for, I could be dead before the sun's down." He shook his head, as if in sorrow. "I reckoned I spelled this out to you, so you could spell it out to your boss. If you didn't, why in hell are you here?"

"When'll I know?"

"When I get good and damn ready to tell you. If you don't like that, go back," Tim said roughly.

"All right, but we're both here. Why don't we keep on this stage?"

"No. I've got some things to write out today. We'll go tomorrow."

Jud finished his drink, not his first of the day, and rose, holstering his gun. He poured another drink, tossed it off, and left the room. Jud, Tim guessed, felt bored, restless and put upon, which was exactly what Tim wanted.

When he went down to eat he was not recognized by either of the women who had served him previously. The beard and the spectacles worked again, and he did not identify himself. He paid for the meal and half the room he was sharing with Jud.

After eating, he went to the store. From the middle-aged owner, who didn't recognize him either, he bought pen and ink, writing paper and a bottle of whiskey. The owner had to fetch the latter from a back room from which came men's voices, among them Jud's.

It was close to dark when Jud came back to the room. From the racket he made climbing the stairs, Tim guessed he was drunk.

Jud opened the room door and halted, a look of surprise coming into his flushed face. Tim had lighted the lamp against the dusk. He had moved the wash basin and pitcher to Jud's bed and, seated in one of the chairs, was using the washstand as a writing table. Several sheets of paper were scattered on his cot. The opened but untouched bottle of whiskey was on the table.

"What in hell's this?" Jud wanted to know.

Tim stood up. "I'll tell you after supper." He moved the papers on his cot into one pile, saying, "How about a drink out of my bottle this time?"

Jud came into the room. "Hell, yes. What else is there to do in this one-jackass dump?" he asked in a slurred voice.

Tim poured a stiff drink into one of the glasses. Supper would help kill its effects, but he wanted Jud just relaxed enough to be unwary after they ate. The triangle, calling all hands to supper, clanged as they finished their drinks.

A big supper sobered up Jud, so that, lighting a cigar up in the room, he was in a relaxed and lazy mood. Sitting on his bed with his back against the wall, he made himself a drink. Tim picked up the papers on his bed and handed them to Jud, saying,

"That's the layout of the car. Tell me how many men we'll have and I'll place them for you."

Jud studied the floor plans of an Adam's messenger railroad car Tim had drawn in minutest detail from memory.

Tim watched him study it before asking, "Ever opened one of those?"

Jud shook his head. "No, banks are easier. Have you?"

Tim smiled and nodded, then moved over to his cot, sat on it, and put his back against the wall. "A half dozen or so. But you'll never believe the easiest."

"Tell me."

Tim took off his spectacles and wiped them with his neckerchief as he talked. "When I was a young'n, always broke, I found out how to get eatin' money: just hang around the depot. When a train came in or passed through, the agent always left his office to pick up a message or send it or hustle baggage. They mostly forgot to lock the door. I'd head for the cash drawer and help myself."

Jud nodded appreciatively. "No railroad where I growed up, though."

"Well, four-five years back I was broke again. I hung around the depot waitin' for a train to haze the agent out of his office. But that time I took more than money. I took some railroad stationery."

"What's that?"

"Oh, writin' paper, with the name of the railroad printed all across the top."

Jud frowned. "What would that get you?"

"That's the whole damn story. I wrote a letter on it. The letter said I was the new night superintendent of the division and to cooperate with me. When the train got goin' I went through to the express car. I hammered on the door until the messenger opened the slot for a look. I poked the letter through to him.

He read it and opened the door. Inside, I buffaloed him and tied him up. I got the safe key off him and loaded the loot in the valise I had along."

"Someone waitin' for you?"

Tim nodded. "At the top of the grade. I just swung off the train and we rode away in the night."

"What'd you get?"

"A little better than five thousand in bank notes."

Jud thought a moment, then said, "Not a bad night's work." He sipped on his drink, and then he laughed. "I'll go you one better'n that. Up in Wyoming, it was. Five of us stopped a U.P. train and cut off the engine and the express car. We made the engineer take the express car a ways up the line. We opened the car with powder and the messenger quit. He opened the safe. We passed up the gold because it's too heavy to carry. But we got us a big bunch of bank notes. Later, when we started sortin' the stuff out, guess what? We had fifty thousand in bank notes and thirty of it was in *thousand-dollar* ones!"

Tim laughed. "Try payin' for a round of drinks with one."

"Yeah. We burned 'em."

How's that, Beth? Tim asked silently. *That was the Ennis job.* Once started, they kept matching stories. Tim drew on his memory of Wanted Files. Jud relied on stories he'd picked up, more often lies than not. But by the time they were past the shank of the evening, Tim had a half-dozen solid leads that Jud detailed so completely that he would have had to be there.

Jud kept drinking steadily. He was pouring his fifth or sixth drink when he regarded Tim seriously. "Just what in hell are we workin' on, Simons? Where and when?"

Tim shook his head. "Not yet, fella. Your friends could be waitin' at any team change ahead."

"They won't be, but damned if I don't wish they would be. You're too close-mouthed for me."

"That's how I've stayed alive. I aim to keep on."

They reached Galena a day and a half later. The town itself was the milling and smelting core of a complex of eight separate and big silver mines in the surrounding mountains. It was ugly, smoky, big, and prosperous. Brick and stone buildings were scattered along its wide main street and its switchyard, down by the river, was a bustle of activity.

The stage edged out of the wagon traffic and pulled up in front of a two-story brick hotel, the Galena House. Jud, first out and carrying his blanket roll, went through the hotel's open doors, looking over his shoulder as he did so. By the time Tim had retrieved his valise from the boot and walked into the lobby and up to the desk, Jud was nowhere around. Tim registered, noting that Jud had written he was from Silver City and had been given room number nineteen. He was assigned room twenty-one.

Because they had agreed to register separately and not from the same place, and because he had registered after Jud, it was up to him to seek out Jud. It had been just short of Galena that he had mentioned this was their destination. Jud had looked shocked and angry, but could not argue among the other stage passengers.

Knocking on the second-floor door of Jud's room, Tim was prepared for anything. Jud opened the door, let him walk in, then closed and locked it behind him. Jud had already brought out the whiskey bottle, which was sitting on the dresser beside a quarter-full glass.

Tim felt Jud's hand on his arm and submitted to being half-turned to face Jud, whose cat's eyes were bright with anger.

Jud said tightly, "Of all the goddamn fool places to get off, this is the worst!"

"Why?"

"It's the county seat, swarming with deputy sheriffs! Besides that, it's headquarters for U.S. Marshal Barry and his crew! Jesus!"

"Any of 'em know you or want you?" Tim asked quietly.

"I don't know! But God, this is like plannin' a bank job in the bank's lobby! You gotta' be crazy!"

Tim smiled faintly, gently disengaged Jud's hand from his arm, walked over to the dresser, and finished Jud's drink. Jud was watching him, his yellow eyes bright with anger.

Tim moved over to the bed and sat on it. "You know, when I was a kid I liked to fish. We lived outside of town, but when I'd go fishing I went into town and fished the river through town. It was the best spot."

"What the hell are you tryin' to say?" Jud asked angrily.

"Just that everybody figured that stretch of river was fished out. They'd head for the mountains or fish below town, but never there."

"So?"

"The marshal and his crew won't be lookin' for you here. They'll be lookin' everywhere *but* here."

The anger began fading from Jud's eyes. "I still don't like it."

"Then stay off the streets." Tim rose. "Me, I'm goin' out."

"What for?" Jud demanded.

"Well, it's none of your damned business, but I'll tell you. There's an old fellow here, Magoffin, used to be an Adam's Express messenger. His car was busted into three times. The Adam's people figured he'd been bought and fired him. He hadn't been bought and it made him mad. He wants to hurt 'em now. I heard about him and looked him up. This job is his idea, and I'm cuttin' him in on my share." He moved toward the door saying, "Want to come along?"

"You said stay off the streets and that's what I'll do."

Tim shrugged. "Want me to bring him here?"

"What for?" Jud asked with his ever-present suspicion.

Tim sighed audibly. "Because he knows the lay of the country. Because he knows the grade that'll slow the train. Because he can draw us a map. Because—"

"All right, bring him," Jud cut in.

Moving past him, Tim said, "It could take some time to find him."

"All right. Just sing out when you knock on the door."

Tim unlocked the door and went out on the busy street. On the way to the county courthouse down the street, he saw many people he knew but who did not recognize this strapping bearded man who wore spectacles. He paused once and stood in the bay of a storefront to scan his back trail for any sign of Jud. He watched the opposite boardwalk, too, and when he was satisfied Jud was not following, he went on. After all, two could play this game of deception.

The red-brick courthouse was so new its bricks had only begun to weather and soot-streak from the railroad and mill smoke. It was a three-story affair, set in a generous lawn with a dozen broad stone steps leading up to its double-doored entrance. Under the steps where they joined the front wall was a doorway, and it was for this door that Tim headed. It let into a basement corridor with an eight-unit cellblock on the left opposite the boiler room.

At a bisecting corridor. Tim turned right and entered the first open door on his left, above which projected a gilt-lettered sign reading U.S. Marshal.

It was a large room, lighted by three narrow and high windows under each of which was a flat-top desk. Against the right wall was a huge roll-top desk and swivel chair. To its right was an American flag in a standard; to its left was a big wall map which two men were now studying.

At the sound of Tim's footsteps on the stone floor, both men turned.

"Yes sir," the older man said, "What can we do for you?"

U.S. Marshal Frank Barry was a tall, gaunt, white-haired man with gray-tufted eyebrows hooding sharp blue eyes. His gray mustache was a full one.

Tim came forward, taking off his spectacles as he did so. He stopped short of the desk and said, "This help you, marshal?"

The marshal stared at him a moment, then his mustache lifted as he smiled. "Good God. Tim Sefton!" He came forward, hand extended, saying, "We'd given you up, Tim." They shook hands warmly. "No word from you, and we were afraid we'd tip your hand if we asked."

The other man, wearing a deputy's badge, came over and shook hands. He was half the marshal's age, a blond-haired and stocky man, and he was laughing softly. "I had you spotted for a schoolteacher, Tim. Man, are we glad to see you!"

"By tonight you'll know what I look like, Jerry, if I can find me a barbershop."

"Sit down, both of you, and let's hear it, Tim," Marshal Barry said.

"Later, marshal. Right now, I've got a man in the room next to mine you'll want to lock up. And believe me, he won't keep. He's so damn spooky he could be gone by now."

"Who is he?" the marshal asked.

"Calls himself Jud Phillips. He's June Constable's number-one boy."

"How—" the marshal began, then said. "All right, let's go." He picked up his hat from the desk. "Come on, we can talk on the street."

"No," Tim said. "I was supposed to bring a man up to his room. He may be across the street to see who I bring. If he recognizes either of you, he's gone."

"Tell us what you want then," Marshal Barry said.

Tim reflected a moment, then said. "If he's across the street, he'll see I'm alone. Maybe he'll wait a minute to make sure I'm not followed. I'll go to room nineteen. If he's there, he'll let me in. If he's not there, I'll go to my own room, twenty-one, and leave the door open. If he sees the open door, he might come in. Whichever room we're in, the door will be locked. All you have to do is listen, because we'll be arguing. Don't knock on either door, because he'll shoot through it. Kick it open and duck away. That'll give me time to move."

"He'll shoot you," Jerry said flatly.

"Maybe. Just one more thing. If you have to shoot, aim for his legs. We've got to have him alive." He put his spectacles back on and said, "Put your badges in your pocket. It he's wearing my badge, pay no mind. Just remember, he's poison. Now give me a ten-minute head start."

As Tim left the marshal looked at the wall clock, then took off his badge and pocketed it. Watching him Deputy Jerry Logan took off his, too, then went to a desk and took out a pair of handcuffs from a drawer.

Tim left the courthouse by the back door, traveled the street behind Main Street for a block, then cut back to it. He crossed the lobby, climbed the stairs, tramped down the hallway, and halted before room nineteen. He knocked firmly and called, "Jud, it's me, Hal."

There was no answer. When he tried the door, it was locked.

Trouble, Tim thought. He moved back to his room

and went in, leaving the door open, the key in the lock. What had happened? Had Jud smelled a trap and run out? He moved over to the window, rammed both hands in his hip pockets, and looked down at the busy street. Where had he gone wrong? *Bringing Jud here,* he thought wryly.

He heard a key softly turn in a lock behind him. Slowly, he turned. Jud, gun in hand and pointed at him, was standing just inside the locked door. His face was tight and bleak as a winter night.

"I'm goin' to gut-shoot you, you bastard," Jud said flatly. "I hope you take a long time to die."

"What's eatin' you?" Tim asked curiously. He suddenly felt his back wet with the instant sweat of fear.

"I followed you. You went to the courthouse—to the goddamn marshal!"

"Of course, I went to the courthouse," Tim answered coldly. "That's where Magoffin works."

"Doin' what? Sheriffin' or marshalin'?"

Tim shook his head in negation. "He's the courthouse janitor, you damn fool. You think he could get a lawman's job after Adam's fired him? He'll be here after work. That'll be around seven, he said."

Jud took a step further into the room and halted, gun leveled and cocked. "You're lyin'!" He was still angry, but the certainty in his voice was fading.

"There's one way to prove I'm not. Go back to the courthouse and ask him," Tim said contemptuously.

"By God, I'll do that!" Jud said flatly. "You'll come with me! Now throw your gun on the—"

Crash! The room door slammed open with a crunch of splintering wood.

Jud whirled, quick as a hunting ferret. A booted leg in the hall was disappearing. Jud shot at it without aiming. Tim was moving already, gun drawn. It took perhaps two seconds for Jud to realize he'd been suckered into a trap and that his back was to his enemy. In that time Tim had drawn his gun and raised it overhead even as he moved. The click of Jud's gun cock came as he began to turn. Tim's gun barrel came down savagely on the base of Jud's skull. In reflex at the shattering pain, Jud pulled the trigger of his gun even as he was falling and the shot went through the floor. Tim was picking up Jud's gun when Marshal Barry and Deputy Logan, guns drawn, came through the doorway and halted, a couple of curious men trailing them.

"You all right?" Marshal Barry asked. Tim straightened up, nodding, and Barry said, "So you didn't have to shoot him."

"No." Tim moved over to the bed, put Jud's gun on it, and sat down. As he watched them handcuff Jud's wrists behind his back he felt a vast sense of relief. He'd come in here in control of a surly bullsnake that, in the last half hour, had turned into an angry rattlesnake.

When, minutes later, Jud was hauled to his feet and slapped into consciousness, his yellow eyes slowly focused on Tim. He said, "You double-crossing son of a bitch, I'll kill you."

Back at the courthouse jail, Jerry Logan, with Marshal Barry watching, ordered Jud to strip. His clothes were searched thoroughly and body and facial scars noted. Jud would answer none of their questions.

Afterward, they adjourned to the marshal's office. Tim and Jerry took the two easy chairs facing the swivel chair the marshall had seated himself in. On his way, Logan had picked up a pencil and a tablet, which he balanced on one knee.

"First thing, what can we hold him on, Tim?"

Tim told of his long session the night at Stone's Ferry, and concluded by saying, "I'm dead sure he was in the bunch that held up the U.P. at Ennis, Wyoming. I'm pretty sure he was on the bank jobs in Grand Forks and Junction City." Logan was taking notes.

"All right, Jerry. Telegraph the commissioner and describe Phillips. Tell him we're telegraphing the Pinkertons for any confirmation they can furnish, especially on the Ennis job. Anything else, Tim?"

"We could ask the Pinkertons if they can tie June Constable into any of these three jobs, couldn't we?" Tim asked.

"Sure. Ask for an answer by wire, Jerry. Tell them a photograph of Phillips follows. Now get going."

Before Jerry had cleared the room, Marshal Barry said, "All right, Tim. Start from when you left here."

Tim told him everything. The old marshal was a good listener—impassive but perceptive. When Tim's account ended with his buffaloing Jud in the hotel room an hour ago, Barry was silent for a long moment. At last he growled, "You're damn lucky to be alive." When Tim only nodded, the marshal was silent again, frowning. Then he said, "A couple of questions, Tim. Why didn't you go back to Mahaffy Station with Jud and put your proposition to June himself? Afraid he'd recognize you?"

Tim nodded, took off his spectacles, pushed them across the desk, and said, "Look through those, Frank."

The marshal picked them up awkwardly, put them on, then looked around the room. Taking them off, he said, "Hell, they're nothing but window glass."

Tim nodded. "If June suspected that, he'd have taken them off and looked through them and said what you just said. Then he'd have told his boys to put a gun on me, yanked off my hat and looked for the scar on my head. He'd have had me cold."

"I believe you. Now for my second question. A while ago you said to shoot at Phillips's legs if we had to shoot, because we had to have him alive. Why do we?"

Tim rose, picked up his spectacles, and began to pace the floor slowly, walking over to the wall that held a bank of file cabinets. He turned, came back, saw the wastebasket beside the marshal's desk, and pitched the spectacles in the basket. The marshal, watching him, smiled but said nothing. Tim went back to his chair and sat down again.

"This has been eatin' at me for more than a week, Frank. At first it was just a notion. When Jud showed up at Stone's Ferry, I thought it might work if we could capture him and jail him without a gunfight."

"What might work?" the marshal asked in a tone of bewilderment.

"Why using Jud as bait to pull June and his bunch up here to bust him out."

The marshal thought on this for some moments, then asked, dryly, "How do we get them here? We can't write them and invite them, or dare them to come."

"Use Sheriff Ben Clay. Telegraph him you've picked up a Jud Phillips on suspicion of murder of a mining-office guard. His companion eluded capture. You found a letter on Phillips addressed to Phillips at Corbett. Ask Clay what he's got on Phillips. Say you'll hold him pending his answer and you'll appreciate any information."

The marshal nodded. "That'd work. Sheriff Clay stalls his answer until June and his men get here. But what makes you think June cares enough about Jud to bust him out?"

"I don't know how much he cares about Jud, but I'll bet he cares plenty about what Jud could tell us about him and his bunch."

The marshal nodded a frowning agreement. "If they come at all, it'll be on a Sunday, I'd reckon. Wouldn't you?"

"Yes. There'd be nobody on the street to shoot at them. Or at night—any night."

"Yes." The marshal rose. "Well, it won't be the first time I've slept in my own jail." He looked at Tim with something close to affection. "You know, I'm glad we're both on the same side. If you were on the other side, I reckon I'd have a hell of a time catching or holding you." At Tim's grin, he said, "You go get your beard shaved off. When Jerry gets back we'll take Phillips over and get him photographed. After that, I reckon I'll telegraph Sheriff Clay and then we sit on our hands and wait for what happens."

10

Tim found the barbershop, bought a bath and hair-
cut, and thankfully had his beard shaved off. Regarding himself in the barbershop's mirror afterward, it
seemed to him that he was wearing a tanned mask
above his cheekbones.

Back at the courthouse, he entered by the door be-
neath the high front steps. As he passed Jud Phillips's
cell, Jud was lying down and at Tim's entrance his
head turned on the cot, and for a moment, he did
not recognize Tim. But then Tim's clothes gave him
away.

Phillips said quietly, "You double-crossing son of a
bitch."

Tim halted, looked at him, and said, "Say that
again."

Phillips repeated his greeting and Tim nodded and
went on down the corridor and into the marshal's office. Jerry Logan was seated at his desk, the closest
one to Marshal Barry's.

"You look some better," Logan said. Then he added,
"At least different."

Tim halted beside Logan's desk and as he took off
his gunbelt, he asked, "Get the photograph of Phillips
for the Pinkertons?"

Jerry nodded. "We can pick 'em up tonight."

Tim laid the gunbelt on Logan's desk top, removed
the badge from his shirt, and laid it on the desk, too.

"Do me a favor, Jerry. Let me in Phillips's cell;
I want a long talk with him."

Logan nodded, reached in the drawer for the cell keys, then led the way back to Phillips's cell in the cellblock. Logan unlocked the door and as Tim stepped into the cell, he said to Logan, "Lock it after me. I'll call you when I want out."

When Logan had left the cellblock Tim walked over to Phillips and halted as the prisoner came to his feet. Slowly Tim peeled out of his jacket, tossed it through the bars into the corridor, and then, hands on hips, regarded Phillips. "I'm not sure I got what you said to me when I came in. What was it?"

"I said, 'You are a double-crossing son of a bitch.'"

"That's what I thought you said," Tim murmured. He moved toward Jud who took a step backward until his legs touched the cot. Into his yellow eyes came a look of uncertainty mingled with disbelief. "You can't—" He never finished what he was about to say.

Tim's right fist drew back and automatically Jud reacted by raising both hands and tucking in his jaw, his eyes watching Tim's right arm. Swiftly Tim moved forward his left fist, driving it into Jud's exposed belly.

The unexpected blow drove the breath from Phillips with an explosive bray. The backs of his knees against the cot, Phillips was pinned there. He fell across the cot, his head rapping against the wall. Immediately he put both hands on the edge of the cot to pull himself up and Tim's deadly right hand caught him square in the throat. Again Jud was thrown back against the wall, but this time he doubled up his knees. The force of the blow drove Jud off the end of the cot so that he fell, face down, on the floor between the end of the cot and the cell bars.

Tim was on him like a cat and as Jud struggled to his feet facing the brick wall, Tim put out a hand, spun him around, and drove his left fist again through Jud's rising guard into his belly.

Cornered now, all Phillips could do was fold his

arms across his midriff and tuck his head down on his chest.

Then came Tim's open-handed stinging slaps at Jud's face, whose head no sooner swiveled left to avoid these heavy slaps than Tim slapped his head the other way. Jud's nose and lips were bleeding as, his arms crossed against his breast, he tried to hug and shrink into himself.

Now Tim reached out, balled up his shirt, and savagely yanked him out of his corner. As Jud passed him, Tim tripped him and Jud sprawled face down on the cell's stone floor.

Tim gave him a thunderous kick in the behind and said, "Roll over and look at me."

Slowly, Jud rolled over on his back with a shuddering groan. His cat's eyes held no anger, only a hurting fear.

"You listenin'?" Tim asked quietly.

Jud nodded feebly.

"I don't mind being called a son of a bitch, but not by you. From now on you call me Mr. son of a bitch. If you don't, this'll happen time and again."

Jud only nodded.

When Tim turned, heading for the cell door, he saw Jerry Logan standing silently in the corridor by the door. Logan unlocked the door and stepped aside to let Tim through. As Tim passed him Logan asked, "He have a nightmare or somethin'?"

"You know, I forgot to ask him," Tim said.

11

For the first three evenings after Tim's departure, both Beth and Dr. Rob avoided each other. Dr. Rob missed an occasional meal and Beth no longer waited until he headed for his Main Street office to walk along with him on her shopping errands. On the fourth evening Dr. Rob was late for supper, so late in fact that Cruz was finished with her own supper in the kitchen and was waiting for her last chores of the evening to begin: this was the serving of supper and cleaning up afterward.

After telling Cruz that she was finished for the day and that she herself would take care of the supper and dishes, Beth said good night to her and heard her tramping up to her attic room. Standing alone in the kitchen, Beth felt a touch of impatience that bordered on anger. Why had the old friendly give-and-take between Dr. Rob and herself ceased and when? In some way she could not exactly pin down, it had to do with Tim Sefton's conversation with them the night before he left. In these last three uncomfortable days both she and Dr. Rob had tacitly avoided any discussion of Tim. It was as if any talk of him by them would be considered an act of disloyalty, so they both had avoided it.

When Beth heard the front door open that evening on the fourth day, she came to her decision.

Dr. Rob called from the living room, "Sorry I'm late Beth, I'll be right down."

When he returned a couple of minutes later, Beth

had their supper laid out on the table. Dr. Rob apologized for his lateness by saying she should not have waited for him and they ate their supper in virtual silence. Afterward, Dr. Rob helped her clear the table and rinse the dishes. Finished with that chore Dr. Rob said soberly, "It is time we had a talk, Beth."

"Yes, you're right. I'll bring our coffee into the living room."

By the time Beth reached the living room with their coffee, Dr. Rob was seated on the corner of the sofa. Beth gave him his coffee, then put her own cup on the table by the window easy chair and sat down.

Dr. Rob began by saying, "Something's come between us, Beth, and we both know what."

"I'm not sure I know, but, yes, something has." Beth said.

"Well, there's not much we can say to each other that we didn't say to Tim the night before he left."

"You think anything we said to him changed him?"

"Not one bit," Dr. Rob said gloomily. He took a sip of his coffee and put the cup down ever so slowly and continued, "Trouble is I like and admire him, but the real trouble is you are half in love with him."

"That's not the same as being in love with him. Half isn't the whole of it."

"What are your reservations, Beth," Dr. Rob asked quietly. "The same as they were the night he left?"

Beth nodded. "He's going to get himself killed, Rob."

Dr. Rob nodded. "Yes, sooner or later." He paused. "Maybe I should say sooner than later. Beth, if you marry him you will be marrying a dead man."

"I know," Beth said bitterly. "If he comes out of Mahaffy Station with the man he's after then he'll be hunting someone else who could kill him."

"Still, he's a clever, careful man."

"He's all that. He's also totally reckless. You told him so yourself."

"Not in those words, but it's what I thought and still think."

Dr. Rob rose, clasped his hands behind his back, made a small circle in the room and hauled up before Beth, looking down at her. "Beth, I want to say something I should have said months ago, because it was true then. I'm in love with you and want to marry you. You never suspected that?"

Beth didn't answer immediately. She watched him as intently as he was watching her.

"Suspected, nothing more. I knew we are more than good friends and always will be. Maybe it took Tim Sefton to open my eyes," Beth said slowly.

"I don't want him to have you, Beth. He'll wreck your life and won't even know he's doing it. I won't. I want us to be married, Beth. I won't pretend I'm anything but what I am. You've known everything about me there is to know—until today. What you didn't know is that I truly love you."

Beth had no answer for that and Dr. Rob knew he had been both stiff and clumsy. He put his hands out, palms up. Beth put hers in his and he pulled her to her feet and enfolded her in his arms. Even the kiss he gave her was not a lover's kiss, but a shy imitation of it. Her kiss was as clumsy as his own. Then he realized with quiet dismay that in his silent courting of her, they had never touched each other. She had taken his arm in their walks together, but that was the extent of their physical contact.

Now he put his hands upon her shoulders and gently eased her back into her chair. Standing before her he shrugged his high shoulders. "God knows what kind of a husband I'll be, but you can be sure I'll make you a loving one. I'm next thing to broke, but I'm a worker and a damn good doctor."

"I think I know why you're next thing to broke, Rob."

Dr. Rob didn't try to hide his surprise. "You do? Why am I, then?"

"Because all those weeks Pearl was in my hospital, you were giving her money so she could pay her room and board."

Dr. Rob said brusquely, "How did you know that?"

"She told me when she paid me yesterday, before the carriage called for her. It was kind of you, Rob."

"Well, she owed you and didn't have the money. After all, she was my patient and I brought her here. She was my responsibility."

"Did she pay you your bill?" Beth asked slyly.

Dr. Rob shrugged. "That's not important, she'll pay me when she can." He frowned. "Why are we talking about her?"

"I thought we were talking about you," Beth said.

"No, we were talking about you marrying me."

Beth slowly shook her head. "Don't make me answer now, Rob. You've just turned my world around. The plain truth is, I need time to think."

"Take it, then. Just tell me when the time's up."

12

It was a gusty fall morning when Sheriff Ben Clay rode into Mahaffy Station. The early snow had mostly melted, although traces of it still remained in the shade of the big pines encircling the sorry-looking buildings. Sheriff Clay was thankful for the sheepskin coat he had put on when he began the climb up the slope to the Ramparts. He dismounted at the store's hitch rail and went inside. Even before the old man, with his black alpaca sleeve guards, moved toward him, the sheriff remembered the entrance into the saloon. He went into the small room, nodded to a couple of card-playing punchers seated at a card table and bellied up to the short bar. Presently the old man came into the barroom, passed behind the sheriff, and came up to him on the other side of the bar.

"What'll it be this morning, sheriff?" the old man asked pleasantly.

Sheriff Clay said, "Don't I know you from somewhere?"

"Corbett. Used to work there for Jim Paulson."

"I remember now," Sheriff Clay said. "Whiskey with a little water."

Sheriff Clay watched him pour the drink and put it before him. He asked then, "Where's June? Haven't seen him since early summer."

"Oh, he got crippled awhile back. He don't hang around the store much now."

"Where can I find him?"

"The big log house next door." The bartender pointed.

The sheriff downed his drink, paid for it, and then retraced his steps to the store porch. He moved down the steps and turned to his right, following the old man's directions.

His knock on the door was answered by June's woman, whom Clay recognized from her monthly visits to Corbett.

"Name's Norah, ain't it? I remember you."

"Yes. Come in, sheriff," Norah said, swinging the door open.

As he went past her the sheriff said, "I'm looking for June."

"He's right in the kitchen, sheriff."

The sheriff saw the kitchen on his right, and moved into it to where June was sitting at the far end of one of the big trestle tables doing some paper work.

June had watched him enter and now called out, "Come on in, Ben."

Clay came over to the table and June rose. They shook hands as the sheriff said, "Hear you got bunged up a while back, June."

"Yeah. Sprung my shoulder." He raised his arm gingerly. "Almost good as new now."

June had a week's growth of beard, but it did not yet fully hide the long scar on his cheek. The sheriff was tempted to comment on it, but June said, "Sit down, Ben, I'll get us a snort."

He rose, went over to the cabinet by the sink, took down a bottle and two glasses, and came back to the table with them. After sitting down he poured the two drinks and said, "I'm tryin' to remember when you was here last, but I can't."

"A little after Mahaffy sold out to you—that puts it back a spell."

They drank. June wiped his mouth on his shirt

sleeve and asked mildly, "Lookin' for someone special, Ben?"

The sheriff said, "Not even lookin', June." He reached into his shirt pocket, brought out a folded piece of paper and moved it in front of June, "Got that early this mornin'."

June took the paper, unfolded it and read:

MAN UNDER ARREST HERE FOR ATTEMPTED MURDER OF MINE-OFFICE GUARD. THE LETTER FOUND ON HIM ADDRESSED TO JUD PHILLIPS, CORBETT. PHILLIPS'S DESCRIPTION FOLLOWS: 6 FEET, 2 INCHES, LONG LIGHT HAIR, CLEAN-SHAVEN, AMBER-COLORED EYES, WEIGHT 180, AGE APPROX. 30-32. DUN GELDING BRANDED /P. MALE COMPANION ESCAPED CAPTURE. IS PHILLIPS KNOWN TO YOUR OFFICE AND CAN YOU CONFIRM IDENTIFICATION? PINKERTONS ARE CHECKING WANTED FILE. WOULD APPRECIATE ANY HELP YOU CAN GIVE ME.

                                MARSHAL FRANK BARRY

June read the telegram twice and the second reading filled him with more wrath than the first. Jud's companion of course was Hal Simons. Whatever mistake they blundered into, Simons had escaped capture. Why had they made any move at all, June wondered? This was supposed to be just a look-see, not the job.

June was aware that Sheriff Clay was watching him. He looked up and regarded Clay's saturnine unreadable face. June said almost idly, "Wire him back that no man answering to that name and description is known in Corbett." He passed the telegram back to the sheriff and said quietly, "Thanks Ben. Now how about sweetening our drinks while Norah rustles up dinner?"

June moved over to the hall and called to his woman in the bedroom. "We're through Norah, come back."

As June returned to the table and poured fresh drinks, Norah came in. While she was setting the table, June's crew began to come in separately until all five of them were gathered. Sheriff Clay knew them all. The fat and dirty one was Russ Overton. Benny Duplessis was the runty, mean-faced one who had skipped Canada. MacSween was older, a big man about June's age. Gavin, a redhead with a bulldog jaw, was even younger than the sleek, handsome Sayres, known only as Duke.

Norah served up the family-style meal of boiled beef, potatoes, and cabbage which ended with great wedges of pumpkin pie.

There was little talk during the meal. What there was of it was trivial. If the men were curious about Sheriff Clay's presence, they didn't show it. To a man, they owed Sheriff Clay a staggering debt of gratitude. He had covered for them on their sprees in Corbett and even let them sleep in his jail when they got too drunk to be taken in at any of the hotels or rooming houses.

When the sheriff finished his cup of coffee, he said to June, "I'm much obliged, June, for the grub. Drop in on me all of you when you're down to Corbett." He rose along with June and June walked with him to the door and said good-bye. In shaking hands, he palmed two one-hundred-dollar bills into Clay's fist. The sheriff nodded his thanks and went out.

Norah was clearing the table and, passing her, June said, "Stack those in the sink and head for your room."

June helped himself from the big coffeepot on the stove, then brought it over and put it on the table. The others helped themselves to coffee after June sat down. When Norah left the room and shut the door behind her, June fired up a cigar. The men fell silent, watching him. Studying the cigar, June sat quietly, then said, "We're in trouble, partners." Now he looked up. "Jud's in the marshal's jail in Galena—

in on a charge of attempted murder." He gave them then the few details outlined from the marshal's telegram to Clay. When he was finished, they were silent, looking at each other.

MacSween spoke first. "What in hell was Jud doin' fighting a mine guard? I thought this was just a scout."

"So did I," June said bitterly. "I don't know if he was drunk or just cut out on his own. Maybe Simons talked him into it. I don't know that, either." He paused, "I do know one thing though. We've got to get him out of there."

The men eyed each other in a sort of shocked silence.

"You mean bust him out of jail?" Duke asked incredulously.

June said flatly, "All right, make a guess, any or all of you. How long will Jud stay locked up before he figures it out for himself? If he talks, if he makes a deal, then they'll go light on him." He looked around the table at each man individually. "There's only one thing he could talk about," June went on. "Us—and what we've done."

"Do you really think Jud would trade?" MacSween asked.

"Given time, any man would." June said flatly.

Duke cleared his throat. "I don't mind riskin' my neck for big loot, but I don't like doin' it for nothin'."

"You were on that U.P. train job in Wyoming with Jud. Want him to trade that?" June asked coldly.

"He won't trade that. He's the one that killed the fireman."

"All right. What about the Granite City bank job?"

Duke only looked sullen, but didn't answer, and June continued. "Jud knows enough about the five of us to hang a couple of us and put the rest in jail for thirty years." He looked around the group. "Either we bust him out or we break up."

Duke asked with disbelief, "You'd leave here?"

"I'd be the first to go. Jud'll blame me for lettin' him rot in jail," June said. "The lot of us will be on reward dodgers in a month."

"That'll bring the bounty hunters flockin' in," Mac-Sween said morosely.

"You can bet on it," June said.

"I'm for gettin' the hell up to Galena in a hurry," MacSween said.

"What about the rest of you?"

He looked at each man individually and they, in turn, nodded their reluctant assent. Duke's nod was almost imperceptible, but June read it as an affirmative vote. June went over to the cabinet, brought out pencil and paper, and returned to the table. Silently he made a sketch of the basement and first floor— labeling rooms, corridors, and cellblock. On a second street of paper, he made a rough drawing of Main Street and the location of the courthouse in relation to other buildings. He handed both sheets and some paper to MacSween and asked, "How many of you know where the courthouse is in Galena?"

Three of the men said they did.

"How many of you know the North Bridge below the courthouse?"

Only Duke was totally ignorant of the town.

"All right, Duke, you travel with Mac. Benny, you travel with Gavin. I'll travel alone. We'll meet under the bridge sometime tomorrow after dark."

"How the hell are we going to move in the dark?" Duke demanded. "We'll be shootin' at each other."

"There's a lamp in that cellblock corridor," Benny Duplessis said. "The jailer won't blow it out, even if you pay him. It's pure hell tryin' to sleep with it. Orders from the sheriff and the marshal. You'll see all right."

"So I've been told, and not only by you," June said. Now he looked at the redheaded Gavin. "Red, you know powder, I've seen you use it. You're the powder man."

"We'll wake up the whole town," Duke objected.

"That's only for an emergency," June said.

"The jailer will have the key or he'll know where it's hid. I don't want a shoot-out with him until Jud's cell is open. When we've got him out we'll split up and this time every man will make it back to here alone. Remember, don't travel the stage roads. Every man packs his own grub and horse feed. Now who's got questions?"

"I got one," Russ said. "You bringin' Jud back here?"

"No chance," June said. "He'll be back sometime, but not soon."

"I got one, too," Duke said. "Don't they lock that courthouse at night?"

"I reckon," June said calmly, "but there's no way you can lock a pane of glass, is there?"

"I hate the hell about all this," Duke said flatly. "Why don't we make it a daylight job?"

"This is Monday," June said. "We'd have to wait until next Sunday to pull it off in the daylight."

"Then wait," Duke countered. "There'll be nobody on the streets then to shoot us up. It beats foolin' round in the dark, don't it?"

"If we had the time that would be easier, but by that time Jud may have figured we're not comin' and he'll start his dickerin'."

"I still don't like it," Duke said.

"If you don't like it, don't go," June said. "Just move your stuff out of here."

"Oh, I'll go, but I sure don't have to like it."

"That's right. You don't have to like it, but you'll do it," June said coldly. "All of you take a look at that first floor drawing of the courthouse. I've put an X on the west wall. That's a hall window where you go in. Keep on down the hall."

The paper was passed around and studied by each man, including Duke.

"You go down those stairs on your right and you're in the cellblock. If there's a jailer there, he won't put up a fight against four men. If there's no jailer, blow the door on Jud's cell. Go out the same way you came in."

"You keep sayin' 'you,'" Duke said. "Where'll you be? Outside?" At June's affirmative nod, Duke said dryly, "Guardin' our rear?"

June said quietly, "Maybe you better pack up after all. Want to?"

"No. I want to go."

June looked at the others. "If there's any trouble at all, it'll come from outside. If four of you can't take care of one jailer, you're in the wrong business."

June rose now, saying, "Any questions?" When nobody answered, he said, "Now let's pack out. Remember—tomorrow night under the bridge."

They filed out and June went into the bedroom. Norah sat on her bed, feet stretched before her, back propped up against the headboard.

She watched him in silence as he opened the closet door, reached in, found his blanket roll, and pitched it on the bed.

"Where you going this time?"

An expression close to amazement came into June's face. "Have I *ever* told you where I was going?"

"No. But someday you won't come back. I won't even know where to look for you."

"When that happens, you'll hear about it." He turned again to the closet, reaching for a heavy shirt.

"June, listen to me for a minute. Just listen."

June threw the shirt on the bed and as he pulled out the tails of the shirt he was wearing, he said, "To what?"

Norah swung her feet to the floor. "Every time you

leave on one of these trips I begin shaking. I shake all the time you're gone."

"Why?"

"I just told you. Sometime you won't come back."

"So what if I don't?"

"I'll have nothing, June. All I own in this world is a half-dozen dresses and four pairs of shoes. Past that, I'll be on my own."

June came away from the closet and sat down on his bed, facing her. "You'll own everything I own," he said in a kind of patient disgust.

"So you say—only say. Have you ever told that to anybody else? Have you ever written it down?" Norah challenged.

"No. Why should I have to? You're the only one I've got to give it to," June said angrily.

"I'm not your wife! You make sure of that! I don't know what you do when you leave here. All I know is that you come home with money you couldn't have earned in the time you were away!"

"That's my business," June said coldly.

"All right. If you're killed or even caught, what happens then? When the people you've robbed find out you have property, what'll they do? Try and get their money back, won't they? I would."

June only stared at her and then asked in a puzzled voice, "What is it you're tryin' to say?"

Norah shook her head. "I don't know. I'm not a lawyer and haven't ever talked with one. But it makes sense—doesn't it?—if a man writes a will leaving his property to somebody, then somebody else can't break that will and take that property."

June stood up abruptly. "Hell, I don't know. I'm no lawyer, either." He walked around her bed and stared out the window. His back to her, he said, "What you want is for me to make out a will in your favor."

"Yes. Has anybody got a better claim?"

He turned and looked at her. "So after I sign you could shoot me in my sleep. Any night."

Norah sighed. "If I'd wanted to do that, I could have done it a long time ago."

"But you wouldn't have got my property," June jibed. "If I sign a will, you can."

Norah rose. "Suit yourself. When you get back from wherever you're going, I'll be gone."

She started toward the door, and June moved around the bed and put himself in front of her. Halting, she regarded him with no expression on her face.

"Where'll you go?" June demanded.

"When you're gone, I'll borrow stage fare from the store money. Don't worry, I'll pay it back."

"I said, where'll you go?"

"Corbett. There's bound to be somebody there that could use a cook or housekeeper. Or a ranch, maybe. I don't know."

"Goddamnit, you'll stay here! Old Dad and Roy won't let you on the stage, I'll see to that."

"All right. Just get yourself a new cook and someone to sleep with. I'm through here. I've quit."

June raised his hand to cuff her and she flinched, expecting it. Slowly then, June's hand sank to his side. The futility of beating her and trying to hold her here against her will suddenly came to him. Somehow, someday, someway, she'd get out of here. Meantime, she'd sulk and slobber around the place, no use in kitchen or bed.

He let her by, changed his shirt, then returned to the kitchen. The whole day, starting with Sheriff Clay's visit, had gone wrong. First the telegram, then the lukewarm reception of his plan to bust Jud out of jail, and now Norah's defiance. Add to that the cold nights and short grub in prospect for the next two days, and he found his mood so savage he knew he must quiet it.

Moving over to the table where pen and ink and

paper still lay scattered on the table, he sat down, put a fresh sheet of paper before him, took up pen, and began to write. Norah did not come near him, but watched him from the other end of the kitchen.

When he was finished, June looked over at her and said, "Come over and read this, Your Majesty. See if it suits you."

Norah came up beside him, picked up the sheet of paper and reading the heading: "Last Will and Testament of Adam Constable, Junior."

As Norah was reading it, Gavin and Russ knocked on the door and came into the kitchen. June ignored them, watching Norah finish reading the will.

"That gives you everything I own when I die. Is that what you want?"

Norah nodded and smiled, and June continued, "I don't know how to write a will, but I damn well know it has to be witnessed." He now looked at the two waiting men. "Come over here and put your John Henry on this, boys."

By three o'clock in the morning, the second night since all had left Mahaffy Station, the last two men, Duke and Gavin, joined June, MacSween, and Benny under the bridge. Russ had been left home to watch the place.

Before they could dismount, June moved over to them and said, "Got the powder and matches, Gavin?"

"Right here," Gavin answered.

"All right. There's a tie rail at the back of the courthouse. Leave your horses there. Come one at a time and keep it as quiet as you can. I'll be waitin' at the window on the west side. I'll go first."

June mounted, crossed the shallow river, picked up the road, and put his horse up the grade.

The town was silent, except for the occasional barking of a dog and the muted racket of a hoist cable from one of the mine's headframes. He did not immediately go to the west window, but kept to the road that ran past the east side of the courthouse. From there, looking at the narrow windows set in the stone foundation of the courthouse, he could see that the cellblock had a lamp burning. Afterward he pulled his horse around and rode it quietly back round the rear of the courthouse and reined up under a dark, high window.

One by one, over several minutes' time, his crew arrived at the tie rail, left their horses, and came over to join him.

When they were all assembled, he said quietly, "I'll break the window. When I'm down, climb up and stand on my saddle. You can reach the window easy from there."

June climbed onto his horse's saddle and braced himself. His chest was just even with the sill of the tall window and he could see the dim light down the corridor that was cast up the stairwell from the cellblock lamp. Now he drew his gun and slashed at the lower pane. It collapsed inside with a loud jangle. June ran his free hand across the wood of the shattered pane, found no shards remaining, and turned and jumped off the saddle onto the ground.

"Inside," he said. He watched until the last man stood on his saddle and pulled himself inside. Afterward he rode his horse to the tie rail, then moved swiftly around the courthouse to the east side. Kneeling by the fartherest of the narrow horizontal windows, he looked into the lamp-lit cellblock.

He could see Jud Phillips through the glass and the heavy wire mesh that covered the window, but he could not see the other cells whose cots were against the wall.

13

As he had done the last four nights, Tim entered the courthouse by the back door, locked it after him, went down the steps, turned left, and entered the Marshal's office. Marshal Barry and Jerry Logan were playing their marathon game of rummy by the light of the wall lamp they had taken from its bracket and placed on the desk.

Approaching the desk, Tim said, "Caught up with him yet, Jerry?"

"It'll take me a year," Logan growled.

Marshal Barry drew a card, put down three threes, and leaned back in his chair. "Town quiet?"

At Tim's nod, he said, "That's the way it goes. These miners get drunk on Friday, Saturday, and Sunday. Monday they dog it, so by Tuesday they're ready to catch up on four nights' sleep."

Tim pulled a chair from behind his desk, swung it alongside Logan's desk, sat down and tossed his hat on the desk, and asked, "Anything new from Phillips?"

Logan smiled. "This afternoon he asked for something to read. I gave him the Bible and he threw it at me."

"He's gettin' pretty edgy, though," the marshal said. "He knows he needs a lawyer, but he won't let us get him one."

"Anybody ask to see him?"

Logan shook his head. "Nope," Logan said. "He

hasn't asked to see anyone either. Maybe he's studyin' to be a hermit."

They speculated on how soon they might hear from the Pinkerton Agency, which had acknowledged receipt of their telegram. All of them knew they were holding Phillips longer than was provided by law. They also knew that any judge would withhold setting him free until the marshal had heard from the Pinkerton's.

Tim knew that the marshal and Logan were as impatient as he was for this situation to get off dead center. He rose now, stretched, and said, "I'm for bed, gents. See you in the mornin'."

He went into the cellblock and took the cell next to Phillips, who was apparently asleep, face to the wall. After peeling off his duck jacket and folding it for a pillow, he took out his gun and put it under the jacket. He took off his gunbelt next and pushed it under his cot. After removing his boots, he lay down on the cot and pulled the blanket over him.

As always when he was alone now, he wondered if his hunch that June would try to free Jud had been a wrong one. The telegram Marshal Barry had received yesterday from Sheriff Ben Clay—saying that no one answering to the name of Phillips or to his description was known in Mineral County—was a lie. That was to be expected. But had he himself guessed wrong on June's reaction to the news of Phillips's arrest? Would June figure that Marshal Barry had lied about Jud's attempt at murdering a mine guard? Was June astute enough to check with the weekly newspaper in Corbett to find out if the Galena weekly newspaper had inquired into the background of Jud Phillips?

There were no certain answers to these nagging questions. When he heard Logan and the marshal come into the two cells beyond him, he turned over and was soon asleep.

A distant sound awakened him and for a few moments he wondered if he had really heard anything. He called softly then, "Hear anything?"

"I did," Logan whispered from the next cell.

The marshal, in the end cell, was gently snoring.

"Get ready," Tim whispered. He reached under his makeshift pillow, found his gun, and cocked it. He heard the muffled sound of Logan cocking his gun. Seconds afterward, he heard the distant tap of boot heels in the hall above. Then came the sound again, and closer. For fear of June recognizing him, Tim had gone to sleep facing the wall and now he inwardly cursed himself for doing so.

The cautious footfalls came slowly nearer and now there was a break in their cadence as they attained the cellblock floor.

Suddenly a voice, loud in that careful silence, said, "Hell, they got close to a tankful."

A second voice close to the first called, "Hey, wake up, Jud!"

Tim rolled over just as Phillips shouted, "Get out! Run! Get out!"

Tim saw four men he had never seen before clustered at the door of Jud's cell. He sat up, raising his gun, but Logan fired the first shot. He had opened his unlocked cell door and was in the corridor.

"Put your hands up and stay where you are!" Logan shouted.

The surprised four knew that they were trapped. Almost in concert they went for their guns, but before their guns were free, Logan shot again.

Tim took aim from his cot, shot, and heard a clang of metal as the bullet hit a cell bar. He lunged from the cot for the cell door just as Marshal Barry let go two quick shots.

Two of the intruders had been knocked to the corridor floor, one still, the other firing his gun. The third and fourth men raced the few feet to the door under the steps and yanked at the locked door, then they turned and started down the corridor toward the stairs.

Aiming through the bars now, Tim took aim at the downed shooter and fired. The man collapsed, arms out in front of him.

Now hugging the cell bars on the corridor side, both Logan and the marshal opened up again.

Phillips stood beside his cot, his lips working, but no sound came out of his mouth.

Tim heard the jangle of glass on the floor of Phillips's cell. Then he heard a shot from outside and he looked up in time to see a gun barrel poked through a hole in the wire mesh of the high window in Phillips's cell. The gun barrel flashed and Phillips, facing the corridor, was driven into the cell bars, steadied himself a moment, then sagged to the floor and rolled over on his back.

The redhead in the corridor now had his hands over his head. Even as Tim watched, the fourth man, shot by either Barry or Logan, wrapped his hands across his chest and pitched to the floor on his back.

The marshal passed Logan on his way to disarm Gavin. Tim pulled his cell door open now and asked Logan, "Any of them June Constable?"

"Constable wears a beard. No."

The marshal reached Gavin, yanked his gun from his holster, and took the sack of powder he had tucked in his belt. Now the marshal backed away and looked through the cell bars at Phillips. He lay on his face in the cell and the bullet hole in his back was streaming blood.

"That son of a bitch shot him apurpose," Gavin said hoarsely, almost unbelievingly.

"Who did?" the marshal asked.

Now Gavin lowered his hands and said, "June. That's why he wanted to stay outside. The murderin' bastard!"

Tim half-turned and then realized that by the time he had reached the stair landing and unlocked the door and got back his night vision, June would have vanished in the blackness.

Logan, reading his thoughts, said, "He's gone, Tim. It's no use."

While the marshal handcuffed Gavin's hands behind his back, Tim and Logan examined the downed men. Two of them—Benny and Duke—had taken chest shots and were dead. Half of MacSween's head was torn away.

Logan opened Phillips's cell and he and Tim turned Jud over. The shot Phillips had taken from the back had torn a gaping hole in his chest and he had died in seconds.

The marshal said, "Jerry, you go wake up old King. Tell him he's got four men to bury. No use wakin' the doc. They're too late for him." He looked at Tim. "Get some lamps lit in the office, will you, Tim? I think this redhead wants to tell us something."

As soon as June saw his shot slam Jud Phillips into the cell bars, he yanked his gun out of the hole he had shot in the screen and ran back for his horse at the tie rail. Mounting him, he held him to a trot until he reached the road that led downhill to the river. Once there, he put his horse in the river and rode him in the stream for a hundred yards before putting him up the bank. He picked up a mine road then and headed south in the quiet night.

Now June's heart had quit hammering in his chest and he began to review what had just happened. He and his men had walked into a planned ambush, of course. The marshal and two of his deputies had posed as prisoners.

The real disaster, he was only beginning to realize, was that he had left Gavin, arms raised against the lawmen's guns, alive and able to talk. It took

June only a few contemplative and bitter seconds before he knew that the redhead surely would talk. He should have taken time to kill him, too. Gavin would reason that June had talked them all into a fool's attempt to break out Phillips. He would be bitter and inevitably he would talk. The more he talked and lied, the fewer months he would spend behind bars.

Patiently now he tried to piece together all the probables involved. First he had to believe that Jud Phillips's story that Beth Avery had let him search her house for Sefton was true. The reason she had allowed the search was that she knew Sefton was safe somewhere else.

Where's your proof? June challenged himself. There was no proof, only a hunch. She was a pretty girl whom any man would covet. She had not only nursed Sefton, but had been willing to lie for him to save his life.

How did Sefton feel about Beth? That was easier to answer. Beth Avery was young, pretty, propertied, and she loved him.

Exactly what was his own situation now? *Mahaffy Station is gone,* he told himself bitterly. *End of the road.* Sefton had suckered him into a trap with Jud Phillips as bait. The word bait lingered in his mind. Slowly, and very carefully, he came to a decision. Tim Sefton could be baited, too.

14

It was well past sunup before red-haired Jim Gavin finished talking from his seat in the chair facing the marshal's big desk. With Tim on one side of him and Logan on the other, Gavin answered all their questions regarding the activities at Mahaffy Station.

At first Gavin talked out of the purest hatred for June Constable. The cold-blooded murder of Jud Phillips was not only shameful, but intolerable to Gavin. From a willing memory he dredged up a score of jobs that June had masterminded and participated in.

Only later, when he had talked himself almost hoarse, did he seem to remember why Jud Phillips had been killed. It was because June was afraid that Phillips would bargain information to the marshal for a lesser charge. Gavin did not know what he would be charged with, but it belatedly occurred to him that he was in a position to bargain, too. When he realized this, his answers to all questions began to be evasive and reluctant. When he finally refused to answer any more questions, the marshal ordered Logan to lock him up.

During the long interrogation, undertaker King and two of his men had taken the dead men out of the cellblock, which they had washed down before leaving.

When Logan and Gavin had left the room, Tim studied the notes he had taken on the interrogation. Marshal Barry was tilted back in his swivel chair, watching the high windows of the office.

Tim closed his notebook and asked, "Where will June head for, Frank?"

"My guess is that he'll get out of the country. Those Pinkerton rewards will add up to big money —so big that half the men in the territory will give up their jobs to hunt him."

"Mexico, maybe?"

The marshal nodded. "Sooner or later, I'd judge."

"No one out of this office can follow him there. Can we?"

The marshal shook his head. "Out of our jurisdiction, Tim."

"What do you want me to do, Frank? Stick around and try to pick up his trail or what?"

The marshal sighed, "Where do you start?"

"He'll need money I'd reckon, but he'll write for that."

"That's no worry of yours, Tim. Your job's done and damned well. June's gang is cleaned out and that's what you came down here to do. You might as well get on back."

"Does it matter if I go back the long way round?" Tim asked.

"Not to me," the marshal said. "Why?"

"I owe a lady in Driscoll a hundred dollars and a hospital bill. I'd like to pay her back in person."

"You haven't got it," the marshal said. He turned his chair around, reached for a piece of paper, scribbled on it and handed it to Tim, and said, "Get that voucher cashed upstairs in the treasurer's office. Then come back and see me."

Tim went upstairs and cashed the marshal's voucher for a month's salary, then went back downstairs to the office. Both the marshal and Logan were waiting for him.

"I couldn't talk you into asking for a transfer here, could I?" Marshal Barry asked.

"I like it here, but I like it up there, too. Besides

Marshal Griffin started me out and I think I owe it to him to stick with him."

"Sure," the marshal said with a tone of resignation. They shook hands all around and the marshal said, "Don't bother turning in your horse; we'll take him to the feed stable along with the dead men's horses. Keep in touch with us, will you?"

Tim said he would and went out into the early morning. It was a bright, cool morning and the town was just coming alive. At his hotel he was the first one in the dining room. Afterward he went up to his room, got his valise, came down and paid his bill. The clerk informed him that the southbound stage was due at the hotel in twenty minutes.

Tim took one of the lobby easy chairs, stretched his legs, and went over the events of last night. While he was pleased that his plan had drawn June and his gang up to this attempted breakout of Phillips, it galled him to think that June Constable was still free. If he wanted to be absolutely honest with himself, he had to admit that he had failed miserably. He had come to capture June Constable, not to help wipe out his gang.

The desk clerk had to come over to wake him for the Driscoll stage.

15

June got into Driscoll the second morning after he had left Galena. After a breakfast in a café across from Cannon's Feed Stable, he led his horse across the street, tied him by the stable, and then went into the stable's office. A bald elderly man, seated at a desk, swiveled his chair around at June's entrance. The two men briefly eyed each other without speaking.

It was June who spoke first. "I hear tell you're a horse trader, Mr. Cannon."

"Who did you hear tell it?" the old man asked cautiously.

"Why it's painted on the side of your stable, ain't it?"

"Yes, you read it. You didn't hear tell about it."

"If you say so," June said. "I aim to buy me another horse and harness for a team and a buckboard."

The old man tilted back in his chair. "Well, I can sell you a horse. There's a harness shop down the street a ways. If you don't mind waitin' a spell, the hardware store can bring in a buckboard."

"Do I look like a rich man?" June asked scornfully. I'm here talkin' second- or third-hand. You either got what I want or I can go somewhere else."

The old man thought a moment, looking past June through the street window. "Oh, I got it all right." His glance shifted to June. "You look like a man with fifty dollars in his pocket. You'll give me fifty and ask for a year to pay. By that time the buckboard'll be wrecked, your dogs will have chewed up the harness, and you'll have traded the horse. You can't pay up, so I take back nothin' but junk."

"This is cash," June said coldly. "If you've got it, let's have a look at it."

The old man sighed, rose, and said, "Come along."

Together they walked down the stable's centerway and stepped out into a tidy wagon yard surrounded on three sides by open-faced sheds under which Cannon's rolling stock was sheltered. There were buggies, buckboards, wagons of all sizes, and even a pony cart.

June walked slowly around the wagon yard, stopping before a light wagon. This would do, but he wanted something that would travel fast. He went on, old man Cannon silently trailing him; then he came to a buckboard that suited him. It had low sideboards and looked to be in sound shape. Afterward, they went out into the big corral. Cannon told the hostler what horses to cut out. One by one, June looked them over and decided on a young bay about the size of his own. He had the hostler take the horse out and gallop him to the edge of town and back, keeping the horse and rider in sight. When they stopped before him, he was certain enough that the horse was not windbroke. In the building again, he bought a satisfactory harness and, while he finished dickering with Cannon, the hostler hitched up the team and threw June's saddle in the bed of the buckboard. June paid Cannon in double eagles, which surprised the old man.

Afterward, June drove up the street, pulled into the tie rail of the grocery store, and bought supplies which the clerk loaded into a gunny sack and carried out to June's buckboard.

Under way again, June drove the team directly to the alley that ran past the Avery place. Remembering when he had last seen Beth Avery, and then only at a distance, she and the doctor had left the house

and gone downtown together around nine o'clock. If
that was the daily pattern of their movements, Beth
Avery had already finished her errands and returned
to the house.

Pulling up in the alley behind the Avery shed, June
tied the team, then stood motionless, anticipating what
he'd probably meet in the next few minutes.

First he was dead certain that the fat Mexican girl
who worked for Beth Avery would recognize him, because she had every reason to remember that he was
the man who shot at Tim Sefton in the hospital room.
If she answered the door and recognized him, he
might be able to frighten her into silence. If Beth
Avery came to the door and let him in, the Mexican
girl would still recognize him. Either way, he had to
shut up the Mex before she roused the neighborhood.

Without hurrying, he rounded the corner of the
shed and headed up the walk that led to the back
porch. Once there he mounted the steps, crossed
the porch, and knocked on the kitchen door. Afterward, he put his back to the door and looked out
as if he were regarding the backyard and shed.

When he heard the door open, he turned slowly
and saw the Mexican girl. He saw the instant rec-
ognition come into her face. Swiftly he drew his gun
and leveled it at her, moving toward her as she
backed away. He said in rapid Spanish, "Don't make
a sound, little one."

Cruz's mouth began to open and she half-turned
as if about to call back into the house.

June raised his gun and brought the barrel slashing
down on Cruz's head.

The girl fell heavily to the floor in spite of June's
attempt to catch her. The thud of her body on the
kitchen floor brought a call from deep in the house.

"Cruz! What's happening?"

June stepped over the fallen girl and moved quickly into the dining room, gun in hand. He was circling

the table when Beth Avery ran into the dining room
and abruptly pulled up. June moved toward her saying softly, "Cruz is all right, Miss Avery. Just stay
you are and keep quiet."

Yes, this was the girl he had seen at a distance—
short, dark-haired, with a full but slim figure. Her
gray eyes were wide with fright.

"Who are you? What are you doing here?"

Still pointing the gun, June said pleasantly, "Why,
Tim Sefton sent me here."

Beth turned her head slightly, saw Cruz sprawled
on the kitchen floor, and then looked at June. "With
a drawn gun? You're lying."

"Yes, I am," June said mildly.

"What is it you want?"

"Your company. Nothing else."

Beth's mouth opened in amazement. "I—don't understand."

June said quietly. "You're coming with me. Be real
quiet. If you yell, you'll get what Cruz got."

"You're kidnapping me, is that it?" At June's solemn
nod, she said, "For ransom?"

"Not for ransom, no."

"Then why?" Beth asked in puzzlement.

"For my own reasons."

Beth was pondering this when they heard footsteps
on the front steps, then on the porch.

"Expectin' anybody?" June asked. When Beth shook
her head, June said, "Don't answer. Don't talk."

Abruptly, then, the front door was opened. June
took a step closer to Beth so he could see who entered.

Dr. Rob came in and immediately saw Beth and
June with gun in hand. The gun was now pointed at
him.

"Close the door and come in," June said with de-
ceptive mildness.

Dr. Rob hesitated, then closed the door behind him, crossed the room, and halted beside Beth.

"Who's he?" June asked Beth.

"Dr. Hasketh. He rooms here," Beth answered.

"And who are you?" Dr. Rob asked brusquely.

"Step away from her and turn around," June said. Dr. Rob did as he was told. June moved over to him, ran his hand down his right side from shoulder to knee; he did the same on the left side, then stepped back. "Turn around," he said.

Dr. Rob turned to face him and now June looked at Beth. Should he shoot the doc? June asked himself. No, not yet, he decided, and inwardly cursed his luck. Now he recalled that Gus had told him the doc was rooming here. *Too late,* he thought sourly. Now his troubles were doubled. It was bad enough to have a bothersome woman on this trip to watch over, but with a man along, too, he was runnin' one hell of a risk. There was only one way to handle that, he thought grimly. Just to keep the doc afraid of what would happen to her.

Now he approached Beth and he shifted the gun to his left hand. When he was close to her, he gave her a swift unexpected clout in the face with the back of his hand, sending her reeling against Dr. Rob. She cried out in pain as Dr. Rob steadied her.

June took a step backward, his gun leveled at the doctor. He saw the anger flare up in Dr. Rob's eyes and read the hatred for him in them.

"You try anythin' funny with me doc and she pays for it. I reckon you know what I mean."

"I do," Dr. Rob said grimly.

"You've got company on your trip."

"What trip?" Dr. Rob asked coldly.

"You'll find out," June said. "Now listen careful. I've got a team and buckboard out behind the shed. You'll be drivin' the team, doc. I'll be settin' behind you, gun

at your back." To Beth he said, "Go get yourself a
warm coat, lassie. You follow her, doc. I'll be behind
you."

Beth led the way through the living room to a
coat closet under the stairs. From it she took a heavy
coat and a black, wide-brimmed straw hat. She put
both coat and hat on and then stood, waiting for directions.

June waved his gun. "All right. Out the back door."

"I don't suppose you care if some of my patients
need me?"

"You suppose right. Now move," June said.

Beth led the way through the dining room, then
when she came to Cruz lying on the kitchen floor she
halted and started to kneel down beside the girl.

"Let her alone," June commanded.

Obediently Beth moved around her and stepped
out on the porch.

Dr. Rob halted too. "What did you do to her?"

"Buffaloed her. Now get on."

"You may have fractured her skull," Dr. Rob said.
"Let me look at her."

"No. She's got so much fat on her, you couldn't
break any bones. Now move."

Dr. Rob joined Beth and together they went down
the steps.

June moved over to the kitchen table, picked up a
straight-backed kitchen chair, and carried it in his left
hand. He paused long enough to ram his gun in his
belt so that his jacket hid it. Afterward, still carrying the chair, he followed Beth and Dr. Rob, a few
paces behind them.

In the alley, June watched while Dr. Rob handed
Beth up into the seat. June came closer then and
swung the chair up into the buckboard and set it up-
right behind the seat.

"Get up," June said to Dr. Rob and watched him
climb up into the seat beside Beth. Then June freed

the reins and came with them to Dr. Rob's side. He said then, "You know where the Corbett Road takes off from Main Street?" At Dr. Rob's nod, June went on, "Travel the street in front of the house here. I'll tell you when to turn. Don't neither of you speak or wave to anyone you see."

He handed the reins to Dr. Rob, climbed up into the buckboard and settled himself into the chair, then said, "Get movin'."

The drive through town drew little attention. The oddity of a man sitting on a chair in the bed of the buckboard could easily be explained by Dr. Rob's presence. Obviously Dr. Hasketh was transporting a patient unable to walk.

In minutes they had crossed Main Street and were climbing into the Ramparts, headed west.

16

It was early afternoon of that same day that Tim's stage pulled up before Cannon's Feed Stable in Driscoll. The stage had nooned at Stone's Ferry. There Tim had asked old man Stone if anyone answering June Constable's description had taken the ferry or stopped at the store. He was told that only a handful of cowpunchers, all known to Stone, had crossed on the ferry. That figured, Tim had thought. June wasn't fool enough to head directly for Mahaffy Station.

Now he headed up the street, carrying the valise, bound for Beth's place. He had a pleasant feeling of anticipation as he left Main Street and took Beth's street. He had much to tell Beth and Rob including, he had to admit, his failure to capture June Constable.

When he was a half block from Beth's house, he noticed that a couple of horses were tied at the hitching block of the Avery house. As he approached the walk to Beth's house, he automatically noted the brands on the two horses and they meant nothing to him.

He mounted the porch, rang the doorbell, and heard someone moving to answer the door.

It opened and he was confronted by Sheriff Davidson. For a moment both men stared at each other and Tim, after his first shock of surprise, said, "Remember me, sheriff? Tim Sefton? I was a patient here."

"Sure I do," the sheriff said soberly and they shook hands.

"Came back to pay my hospital bill," Tim said. "Beth around?"

Sheriff Davidson opened the door wider and said, "You'd better come in, Tim."

Tim took off his hat and walked past the burly sheriff, then turned as Davidson shut the door.

"Anything wrong?" Tim asked.

"About everything that could be," the sheriff growled. "Beth and the doc are missing."

"What happened?" Tim asked.

"Come on back. We're talking to the Mexican girl." As he headed for the kitchen, he asked over his shoulder, "You speak any Mexican?"

"Some," Tim answered.

"Then talk to her. She come down to the office about a half hour ago. I can't make any sense of what she's saying."

Tim followed the sheriff through the dining room and in the kitchen halted beside him. Cruz was seated at the kitchen table across from a young deputy, who rose at their entrance. Cruz had been crying and she was still sobbing. When she saw Tim, she tried a smile that did not quite come off.

Tim walked over to her and she rose and they shook hands. That started a fresh torrent of tears from Cruz whose dress-front was wet from earlier weeping.

Tim gestured for her to sit, and then he sat down in the chair that the deputy had vacated.

Tim said in Spanish, "I know you are sad Cruz, but tell it from the beginning."

Cruz opened up in a torrent of Spanish. Tim held up his hand, palm out, to stop her. "Slowly, now."

"This man knocked on the kitchen door and I opened it. His back was to me. He was looking at the shed. He heard me and turned. He is the same man! I swear it!"

"The same man as who?" Tim cut in.

"The same man that shot at you here! When you were sick!"

"You are sure of that, Cruz?" Tim's heart was suddenly pounding.

The girl nodded emphatically. "The voice was the same. He speaks Mexican like one of us. His beard was not so thick as before, but he is the same man."

"Good. Then what happened?"

"He pointed his gun at me and said, 'Don't make a sound, little one.' I turned my head to call Miss Beth. He hit me on the head. I saw many lights and it hurt."

"Then what?"

"I was asleep. When I woke up, I heard people talking—him to Miss Beth. I was lying on the floor. I didn't move because I was afraid he would shoot me. I kept my eyes shut and listened. He was going to take her away when the doctor came in the front door."

She was silent, frowning, making an effort to remember. Tim said nothing, afraid that anything he might say would sidetrack her. Sheriff Davidson and his deputy were silent, too, watching the girl and only catching an occasional word.

Cruz finally picked up her story. "I don't know why he slapped Miss Beth, but he did. Then he told them he had a wagon in the alley. He told Miss Beth to get a warm coat. Miss Beth stopped beside me to see if I was all right. He told her to go out. The doctor stopped by me, but he sent him out, too. He took a chair like you're sitting in and carried it out. That's all I know."

"You went downtown to get the sheriff afterwards?"

When Cruz nodded, Tim rose and said, "Go in

and lie down, Cruz. Get some rest." He smiled at her. "We'll find them."

To the sheriff, he said, "Let's talk in the living room."

The three men moved toward the front of the house, while Cruz went into the bedroom off the kitchen. In the living room Sheriff Davidson and his deputy sat down on the sofa and Tim took an easy chair facing them. Davidson said to his deputy, "Go on back to the office, Dave. Somebody's got to mind the store." The disappointed deputy left.

Then Tim told the sheriff what Cruz had told him —that indeed June Constable from Mahaffy Station was the kidnapper. Tim had to backtrack and tell him of the attempted breakout of Jud Phillips at Galena by June and his men.

"He runs the store there at Mahaffy Station, don't he?" the sheriff asked. At Tim's nod, the sheriff went on, "Seen him a couple of times, but don't really know him. He'll likely stay away from there for a while."

"Anything strike you as strange in Cruz's story?"

"It's all damn strange. What struck you?"

"Constable told Beth to get a coat. Why would he?"

"Well, the nights are gettin' nippy," the sheriff offered.

"The days are nippy, too, up in the Ramparts."

"You think they'll head for Mahaffy Station?" the sheriff asked doubtfully. "He wouldn't be that big a fool, would he?"

"No, but I aim to find out."

"*We* aim to find out," the sheriff corrected him.

"No. Just me. He's out of your county, sheriff."

"She was kidnapped in my county, wasn't she?" the sheriff countered.

This is a good lawman, Tim thought. *Willing and able to help, but no thanks.*

The sheriff misinterpreted his silence. "If there's a reward out for him, I wouldn't claim any part of it."

"It's not that. No U.S. Marshal or Deputy Marshal is allowed to accept reward money. Not from the Pinkertons or anybody else."

The sheriff shrugged his heavy shoulders. "I'm only offering to help. How can I?"

Tim suddenly realized he was angry, and for no apparent reason. Searching for the cause, he thought he had it. The sheriff deserved an honest answer. Tim said, "You can help me most by leaving me alone, sheriff."

He saw the anger flare into the sheriff's eyes as he prepared to rise. "That, I'll do," Sheriff Davidson said.

"Wait," Tim said gently. He rose, started for the dining room, halted, and came back to stand in front of the sheriff.

"This doesn't make sense, but maybe you can understand," Tim said. He paused, wondering how to say this. "Look, I own June Constable. He's mine to kill and I will. Make sense?"

"Not yet."

"To begin with, he drygulched me and left me for dead." When the sheriff nodded, Tim went on. "When he was sure I was alive he came to this house to finish the job. That's two times. The third time was when he sent Phillips to gun me down. Beth hid me."

"I didn't know that."

"Believe it—believe this, too. I was sent down here from Colorado by my boss. I was on loan to Marshal Barry for just one reason: I was a new face that June Constable had never seen. My job was to arrest Constable and his gang of hardcases. I've told you about that."

At the sheriff's nod, Tim continued, "We got them all but Constable, so I failed. When I say I own him I mean just that. He's mine. I'll bring him in alive or dead. Is it beginning to make sense now?"

"Kind of." The sheriff thought a moment. "That alive or dead works both ways don't it?"

"It could, but it won't. Like I said, I own him."

The sheriff rose. "All right, he's yours. I think you're makin' a mistake, though."

"Not the first one," Tim agreed. He extended his hand and the sheriff took it. "Thanks for your offer and for everything you've done."

"A question," the sheriff said. At Tim's nod, he went on. "Why do you think he'd wait for you at Mahaffy Station?"

"He knows that country like the back of his hand. Where else could he go and feel as safe as he does there? In another week, there'll be reward dodgers out with a price on his head. Any man driving a team with a pretty girl alongside him will be stopped and questioned. He's purely safe there and he knows it."

The sheriff nodded. "Good huntin'."

The sheriff went out and Tim, at the window, watched him ride off. Afterward, Tim silently prowled the living room, reviewing what Cruz had told him. There was no doubt in his mind that June was headed for Mahaffy Station. For him to go anywhere else made no sense at all.

The kidnapping of Dr. Rob was an accident. Tim knew June couldn't kill him here and the only alternative was to take the doc along with Beth.

Other things bothered him, too. Where had June got the wagon? While Tim was certain that June was headed for Mahaffy Station, he couldn't afford to be mistaken. Somebody was bound to have seen the odd sight of a man seated in a kitchen chair on the bed of a wagon being driven through town.

Tim moved back into the hospital room, stripped both beds of their blankets, and made them into a blanket roll. Moving around to the back porch, he took down the short clothesline and with it secured the blanket roll. Then he went back into the house and looked in on Cruz, who was sleeping. Afterward, blanket roll over his shoulder, he went out into the alley and read what the tracks there told him. He followed the tracks down to the cross-street, where later traffic had erased them, and then headed for Cannon's Feed Stable.

In the feed-stable office, while he was waiting for a horse to be saddled for him, he asked old man Cannon if a man had been in the office earlier to rent or buy a light wagon. The old man confirmed that a man had bought a horse, buckboard and harness, and had paid in gold eagles.

Tim paid for a week's rental of a horse and saddle and afterward went out into the corral, adjusted the stirrups of his rented saddle, and tied his blanket roll behind the cantle. Mounting, he rode through the sparse wagon traffic to the bank, on a corner three blocks up Main Street.

Tying his horse in front of the bank, he crossed the street and went into the big and shabby saloon named The Liberty. The saloon was almost idle at this hour and Tim inquired of a bartender if he had seen a buckboard carrying three people, one seated on a kitchen chair behind the buckboard seat, drive past the saloon before noon.

The thin, melancholy looking bartender abruptly smiled at his question. "I never seen it, but old Joe, the swamper, seen it and told me. Said a man was sittin' in a house chair behind the seat makin' out like he was a king or somethin'."

"Which way was it headed?"

"Into the mountains," the bartender said. "I'll bet he's got a real sore tail by now."

"Where do I find old Joe?"

"If he ain't sweepin' the walk out front, he's rollin' out empties in back. Go on through; you can't miss him."

Tim headed back down the bar and passed through a corridor on both sides of which were private card rooms, their doors open to air out last night's tobacco smoke.

On the loading platform at the end of the corridor, he found old Joe, a near-toothless and hairless old man, who was midway through rinsing out a dozen battered, brass cuspidors. At sight of Tim, the old man leaned both elbows on the edge of the washtub and asked pleasantly, "Lookin' for someone?"

"You," Tim said. Then he put the question to the old man about seeing a buckboard earlier in the day which held a woman and two men, one of which was seated on a kitchen chair.

Joe chuckled. "Thought I was drunk, but it was too early for that. That-there man figgered he was king of the mountain. He never looked anywhere except straight ahead. Damn silly, if you ask me."

"Maybe he was crippled. Which way was the team headed?"

"Into the mountains. I watched it for a block and it took the Corbett Road." He reflected a moment and said, "Why didn't he take the mornin' stage?"

"I don't know, old-timer. His choice, I reckon." Tim gave a careless wave and a gesture of thanks and headed back for his horse. He had proof now that June, Dr. Rob, and Beth were headed in the direction of Mahaffy Station, perhaps beyond, but he doubted that.

17

The long haul up the Ramparts was like nothing Dr. Rob Hasketh had ever experienced. To begin with, the man who was kidnapping them was a stranger to him. Although, as the team labored into the chilly high country, he had made a guess. Whether or not it was a correct guess he didn't know, for every time he tried to speak to Beth or their captor he heard a growled, "Shut up," and felt the cold barrel of a pistol in his neck. When Beth tried to talk, the pistol was at her neck. There was no conversation among the three of them for most of the long trip.

In that silence, broken only by the rattle of the buckboard on the rough, rocky road, Dr. Rob pondered what lay ahead for Beth and for him. If this man was June Constable, as he suspected only because he knew they were headed for Mahaffy Station, then what did Constable hope to gain by seizing Beth? He knew that he himself was of no interest to Constable; he had simply interrupted a situation that forced Constable to bring him along. It was Beth that Constable wanted, but why? What did he propose to do with her? For most certainly when Cruz regained consciousness, she would sound the alarm and this whole part of the country would be on the alert for them.

It took Beth to finally break the silence. She turned in the buckboard until she looked at June and said, "That pistol doesn't scare me. If you were going to shoot me you'd have done it hours ago."

June neither spoke nor pointed his gun at her.

She now asked Dr. Rob, "You know who he is?"

"June Constable, I'd guess."

Beth looked again at June. "Are you?"

"My turn to keep my mouth shut," June said dryly.

"What do you want with me?"

"It don't matter," June said. "But it'll be a surprise, though."

Dr. Rob asked then, "You expect to get away with this, Constable?"

"I have so far, and I don't see anything ahead to stop me."

There was really nothing more for any of them to say, the doctor thought. If he begged for Beth's safety, he would be talking to a man whose mind was already made up and locked shut. Still, he persisted. "What happened up in Galena?"

Silence.

There were other questions he could ask, but he knew they would not be answered. Neither would any question that Beth asked him, Dr. Rob was certain. The improbable stage was already set and he and Beth would act their roles as directed.

There was a light covering of snow on the ground now and it held the marks of the early stage. Shortly afterwards the road leveled off and presently the black timber fell away and they were in the big open park that held the buildings of Mahaffy Station. Both Beth and the doctor regarded the drab store and the buildings beyond them. Smoke from the half-dozen chimneys and stovepipes made a high blanket in the still, cold air. The shabby settlement looked abandoned and there was not a horse at the store's tie rail.

"Pull up at the blacksmith's shop by the corral," June directed.

The sound of the approaching horses brought young Roy from the interior of the blacksmith shop. He halted just outside it and stared at the buckboard and the two strangers and then saw June.

"See that big house by the store? Go over to it and go inside," June said.

The doctor climbed down stiffly, walked around the horses, and gave Beth a hand to steady her as she climbed down.

June left his chair, stepped over the seat, and nimbly dropped to the ground.

Roy approached him now and June said, "Hiya, boy."

"What kind of a crazy rig is that, June?" Roy asked.

"Just what it looks like, son. Now listen. Go find Russ and send him to the house. Then unhook and feed the team."

Roy nodded. "Where's the rest of the bunch?"

"Likely still drinkin' in Driscoll," June said easily. "Now go find Russ."

June skirted the team and headed for the big log house, Beth and Dr. Rob twenty yards in front of him.

That damn doctor had surprised him back there in Driscoll, but it had all worked out. He had what he wanted and that was Beth Avery. She was a spunky one all right, but he'd break her of that quick enough.

Beth and the doctor had halted in front of the house door and were waiting for him. He passed them, opened the door, called, "Come in," over his shoulder and went inside.

They followed him into the big kitchen and he waved to a table. "Sit down," he ordered.

Norah came in through the hall from the bedroom, saw June, smiled, and then looked at the strange man and woman who were seating themselves on the bench alongside the table.

"Feed us somethin' in a hurry, Norah."

June made no attempt to introduce the doctor or Beth and Norah seemed not to expect him to. As she passed him headed for the stove, June gave her an affectionate slap on the rump.

Afterward, June went to the cupboard and lifted out a bottle of whiskey and three glasses which he brought back to the table. Standing at the head of the table he poured each glass half-full of whiskey and said, "Drink it if you want it."

Dr. Rob looked at Beth inquiringly and when she nodded, he moved a glass before her, then took the second glass. June, still standing, drank his drink, then refilled his glass and sat down.

Beth and Dr. Rob looked at each other and Dr. Rob shrugged, lifted his glass, nodded to Beth and waited until she had tasted hers before sampling his own. The strangeness of their reception or rather lack of it was baffling. The woman of the house had looked at them without curiosity or even acknowledgment. It was almost as if she knew who they were and was expecting them.

June made no attempt at conversation, so they, too, were silent.

The outer door opened, then closed, and a heavy-set, dirty and unshaven man, his hat still on, stepped into the room and caught sight of June.

June picked up his drink, said, "Hi, Russ." Then he took Russ by the elbow, and both moved through the short hall and into the bedroom. He closed the door behind him and then said, "From now on, you've got one job, Russ, until I tell you it's over. You'll stick to that man in there. He'll be here, I don't know how many days, but you or Roy will be beside him around the clock. Keep him away from all guns."

Russ thought a moment, then said, "You mean if he gets aholt of one, he'll shoot me?"

"For sure," June said quietly. "This is his jail; you or Roy are the guards. If he makes a break, kill him."

Russ nodded. "What about the woman?"

"No concern of yours. Norah will watch her."

Russ nodded. "I'd rather look at her, but it's him I'll watch," he said in agreement.

"From now on, Russ. From this second on, until I tell you to quit."

At Russ's nod of acknowledgment, June took a sip of his whiskey and went into the kitchen, Russ following. In the kitchen Russ went over to the second trestle table, took off his hat, and sat down. Norah, at the stove, was ladling stew out of the kettle that fed the crew at any hour of the day or night. Of the three plates on the counter beside her, she filled only two, then took them over and placed them before the doctor and Beth. She had set the table while June and Russ were conferring.

June was slowly pacing the floor and sipping at his whiskey. Norah moved over to him now and he halted, eying her with a questioning glance.

"Not feedin' me?" he asked.

"Not yet," Norah answered. "Come along," she said then and headed for the bedroom.

June followed her into the room, closing the door behind him. Norah sat down on the nearest bed and pushed strands of her graying hair from her forehead. When she looked at him, June saw an unaccustomed chill in her usually mild blue eyes. It alerted him.

"What are you goin' to do with them?" Norah asked.

"Keep them and feed them."

"Are they payin'?"

"You could say that. Yes."

"Why are they here, anyway?"

June thought a moment, then said, "I never told you about Tim Sefton, did I?"

"You never tell me anything. No, I never heard the name."

June was brief and to the point. He told her of his letter from Dock, who warned him of Sefton's hunting for him. He described, with no details whatsoever, his attempt to drygulch Sefton, his failure, and his attempt to murder Sefton in Beth Avery's hospital. He also described Jud Phillips's attempt to find Sefton and of his failure.

Norah listened patiently, reflecting no surprise at what June had just told her. Violence was his way of life, and long ago she had accepted it.

What surprised her was his telling of the events in Galena, disclosing the deaths of four men she had known and fed and whose clothes she had washed for close on to four years.

"You haven't said anything about Gavin," Norah said.

"He quit, hands in the air."

"He'll talk. What's he got to lose if he tells about us."

"You're finally catching on," June said dryly.

"I haven't caught on yet," Norah said tartly.

"Sefton baited me up to Galena and Jud was the bait. I'm baitin' Sefton up to here."

"Because he's in love with Beth Avery?" Norah said as if she had guessed it all along.

"Now you've caught on," June said.

"Aren't they looking for you now?"

June nodded. "Sure, they are, but I was never in Galena; nobody saw me."

"But Gavin knew you were there."

"*He* says," June said contemptuously. "*You* say I was here for the past month."

"It won't work," Norah said.

"It'll get Sefton up here. That's all I care about."

"So you kill him. Then what?"

"You still don't savvy this. All I want is to draw Sefton here. Afterwards I can take care of myself. I always have, haven't I?"

"How soon and where?"

"Three-four days, maybe. I don't know, but he'll be here."

"Where do you go?"

"Mexico, likely."

"With me?"

"No chance. None at all."

"With her?"

"Good God, no! The last thing I want with me is a woman."

"What happens to me? You're gone for a month, maybe two, maybe a year, maybe ten years."

June gave a sigh of exasperation. "I signed everything over to you, didn't I? You've got the store to feed and dress you. You've got cattle and booze, too. What else do you need, short of a trip around the Horn?"

"In plain words, you're leavin' me," Norah said.

"Did I ever promise I wouldn't?"

"No, you never, but I guess I'll make out."

"Almost as good as I did, maybe better."

"This is all because of Tim Sefton?"

June only nodded.

"They're bound to be after you, aren't they?"

"For sure."

"Then they'll arrest me for helping you. There goes the store and the house and everything else." She paused, then added, "Thanks for nothin'—an awful lot of nothin'."

"That's what you came with. Remember?"

"Too well," Norah said bitterly. "Just nine years out of my life and you throw it away out of your stud's pride."

June took a step toward her and hit her with his open hand. It was a swift, savage blow and because it was unexpected it caught her unawares. It knocked her first on her back, then, because of its violence, it turned her on her side and she fell between the bed and the wall and landed on all fours, face down.

She crouched there for some five seconds and then came slowly to her feet.

"You goddamn *idiot* sow! You're my common-law wife. They can't make you talk and they can't arrest you for anythin'. You know all that, so what's behind this crybaby stuff?"

"I want to go with you," Norah said quietly.

"If you do, you'll kill us both. No! Now feed me, I'm hungry."

Norah went past him and he followed her into the kitchen. Taking his seat at the head of the table, he noticed that his two captives had finished eating. They had doubtless talked together about their situation in voices too low for Russ to hear. The determined look behind the doc's spectacles confirmed this.

Norah brought his plate of stew and June began eating. Rob let him get the edge off his hunger and then asked quietly, "What do you plan to do with us?"

June swallowed a mouthful of stew and then said, "Keep you here three-four days."

"You can't!" he said angrily. "I left a woman just about to begin labor. I left a man with gangrene. If I don't dress his leg, he'll lose it."

"They got along without you before you come. They can do it again," June said calmly.

Dr. Rob looked at Beth, then regarded June again. "Why are we here, anyway?"

"You're here because you walked in her house at the wrong time. She's here because I figure somebody'll come after her."

"Who?"

Beth said, "He means Tim, Rob."

"What if he does come?" the doctor asked.

"I'll kill him."

There was a short silence before the doctor asked, "For no reason at all except he suckered you up there?"

"That and killin' four of my men."

Russ came alert now. Roy had told him the boys

were drinking in Driscoll. Was June lying to this man?

"I think you're lying," the doc said. "And you won't kill him if I can help it."

"You can't," June said. "Show him, Russ."

Russ rose from his bench, drew his gun as he took a step, then with the flat of his gun clouted Rob with a sideswipe to the side of his head.

Dr. Rob's glasses were knocked onto the table and shattered by the blow. The force of the blow drove him sideways into Beth who was tumbled backward off the bench. Rob helped her to her feet, then turned to look at the two men.

His voice was choked with fury as he said, "You miserable bastards! I can't see without those glasses, and you've broken them!"

"What's there to see?" June asked with indifference and resumed eating.

18

It was long after dark when Tim reined up where the timber broke away for the Mahaffy clearing. There were a couple of lamps burning in the distant cabins. The high cloud cover here obscured the stars and the Big Dipper whose handle had been his night clock since childhood. With no notion of the time, he couldn't tell if the lamps were night lights or whether some people here were still awake.

Sitting in the saddle, letting his horse blow, he had the certain feeling that to ride into Mahaffy Station now would be the height of foolishness. The dogs would pick up the sound of his horse moving on the frozen road and would pass on the alarm, warning June that there was a rider out here in the night.

He moved his horse into the timber and let him pick his way south until they were well away from the road. Here he stopped, grained his horse by feel and picketed him, then took down his blanket roll. He was due for a cold night, he knew, but he couldn't risk a fire.

When he had quit shivering in his blankets he found that, tired as he was, he couldn't sleep. His night thoughts then turned toward the next morning. The first order of things was to make sure Beth and Rob were being held here. If they were, how to get them out? *So I'm June*, he thought. *How do I bush-whack a man here?*

Remembering his stage ride back from Corbett to Driscoll, he recalled the cabins, the big house, the store, the blacksmith shop, and the barn—any of them ideal for hiding a man bent on ambush.

But would June be expecting him this soon? Tim thought not. He might be expecting someone from Driscoll looking for Beth and the doc, but since he didn't intend to kill the questioner all he had to do was say they weren't here. In other words, he would go about his usual routine for a few days, then prepare his ambush.

Was this good reasoning? He was too tired to know. Presently, he slept.

A strip of jerky in one hand, his canteen in the other, Tim watched Mahaffy Station come awake. He was seated, his back against a tree, chewing hungrily on the jerky, with a clear view of the settlement below him. He watched the smoke from the first fires lift into the chill gray sky; he watched people head for privies; he saw hay forked from the barn loft to horses in the corral; he smiled as he observed each dog get reacquainted with his friends after a long night's absence. Mostly, he watched the big log house.

He was again speculating on where June would set up his ambush when two women came out the door of the big house. The first woman he didn't recognize; the second was Beth. Together, they walked around the corner of the house and were lost to sight. Tim felt a grim satisfaction at the sight, for he had read June's move correctly, just as June had surely read his own. Kidnap Beth and when Sefton came to get her, kill him. June had used Beth precisely as he himself had used Jud Phillips, Tim thought wryly.

He watched the women return and go inside the house. Some minutes later the door opened again and Dr. Rob stepped out, tripping over the doorsill but still catching his balance. Behind him came a big-bellied guard, the same man he had slugged in the

Union Saloon in Corbett. He took Rob's elbow and together they walked around the corner of the house
and disappeared. Rob drunk? And at this hour? Tim
knew better; Rob had lost or broken his glasses.

Now Tim sized up the situation with a growing dis-
like of it. He knew Beth and Rob were here. He
thought June wouldn't expect him yet and would not
have prepared his ambush. Then why not hit now?

As he watched, he saw an older man and a younger
one approach the blacksmith shop from the west.
They disappeared into the blacksmith shop.

Do it now, Tim thought. He rose, went back to his
horse, and stripped off the saddle he had put on him
two hours back. Leaving the horse tied to a tree, he
slung the saddle and bridle over his shoulder and
went back to where he'd been watching. He passed it
and started down the gentle slope, aiming for the
blacksmith shop, saddle still over his shoulder. He
kept an eye on the big house as he made his leisurely
way down the grade, reached the corrals, moved
parallel with them past the barn, and came to the
blacksmith shop. Its double doors were open and he
could hear activity inside, and men talking.

He moved with seeming weariness into the doorway, and gave a brief glance at the single big room
which was lighted from a lone window on the corral
side. The young man and the old man ceased talking
as Tim slowly slacked his saddle to the ground, saying,
"Man, am I glad to be here."

"You afoot?" the old man asked. He and the younger man ceased their work on the harness they were
holding.

Tim came wearily over to the forge, hands already
extended for the warmth of its coals. "I sure as hell
am." He stopped at the forge.

"What happened to your horse?" the young man
asked.

"Well, I was comin' up from the south, headin' for

Corbett. Didn't have no business in Driscoll, so I figure to cut the corner and head straight for the Pass."

"Nobody ever tell you that's canyon country?" the old man asked.

Tim smiled forlornly. "No, but I sure found out. Made camp in a wet one close to dark. Staked out my horse on some grass, et, and rolled in my blankets. The horse woke me up fussin'. 'Fore I could get to him, he pulled out, stake and all. Then I heard them big cats talkin'. That's what spooked him. Never knew them big cats worked at night."

"If they're hungry, they'll work any time," the old man said.

"I don't reckon that horse has quit runnin' yet. I figgered that rope'd hang him up somewhere, but it never."

As he talked Tim noted that neither man was carrying a gun which would only be a hindrance to them in their work. A rifle might be in a back corner, but they were unarmed. Tim had positioned himself now so he could see the log house and the store. Nothing moved out there.

"You musta been hoofin' it most of the night," the old man observed.

Tim nodded. "The longest and coldest night I can remember. Any place a man could get a drink around here?"

"There's a saloon in the store," the young man said.

Tim nodded and looked from one to the other. "You fellas can use an eye-opener on a cold mornin', can't you? Me, I don't like to drink alone."

The young man looked at his partner. "Go ahead, Dad, I can take care of this." He held up the harness.

"Sure you can, Roy. I won't be long."

Dad joined Tim, who put the old man between the house and himself. If June were not watching too closely, it would appear that Dad was headed for a

drink with a friend, not the marshal June was waiting
for. All hands here would be alerted to report a
strange rider, Tim guessed. A horseless cowboy
wouldn't be worth reporting, he hoped.

Dad said, "The boss don't mind if we take off for a
drink when things ain't busy. But let him catch you
with a bottle in the place and you're on your way."

"That makes sense," Tim said idly. He was watching the house, ready to move if the door opened.

They crossed to the store porch, Dad leading. Tim
looked over his shoulder then and saw with shock
that Roy was heading for the log house next door.
He wasn't hurrying, but what business did he have
there at this hour unless it was to report a stranger?

They went inside the store and turned left, heading for the saloon. From the back of the store a
pleasant voice called, "Pour your own, Dad. I'm working on the books."

Dad led the way to the bar. Tim looked past him
and saw the bolted back door. As Dad rounded the
bar, Tim said, "Make mine a big one, Dad. I'll be
back."

He headed for the back door and was unbolting it
when Dad's voice, suddenly iron, said "Turn around."

Tim wheeled. The old boy had lifted the sawed-off
shotgun from under the bar; it now lay on the bar,
pointed at the back door and Tim.

Tim slowly reached into his shirt pocket, brought
out his marshal's badge, and held it up. He said gently, "Put it back, old man, and I'll forget I ever saw it.
Remember, there'll be two witnesses to this—my witnesses. Prison's no place to die in. Now put it back,
and pour two drinks."

The old man opened his mouth to speak, thought
better of it, lifted the shotgun and was putting it
back under the bar as Tim turned, unbolted the
door, and swung it open.

He was so close to the house—fifteen yards perhaps

—that he had to flatten his back against the outside wall to keep from being seen from the kitchen windows.

He drew his gun now. Since he couldn't see the door, he had to rely on sound. Now he held his breath, hearing only the wild pounding of his heart.

The first warning of movement was the sound of running feet coming toward him. Raising and cocking his gun, he waited.

In less than three seconds, fat Russ, gun held out in front of him, pounded around the corner. At sight of Tim and still running, he shot without aiming and missed. Tim's shot simply echoed his, and he did not miss. The slug half-turned Russ and his gun went sailing out of his hand. He landed on his side with a driving, earth-pounding lunge.

Tim moved to the corner, squatted, took off his Stetson, raised it over his head and edged its brim around the corner. A shot from a rifle punctured the brim. Swiftly Tim moved around the corner, gun cocked.

He saw two happenings at once. June, hatless and out in the open facing the corner, was pumping a reload into his carbine. Rob was backing out the door, shouting, "Don't! Don't!" he tripped on the doorsill and fell flat. Tim raised his gun and was taking careful aim as the young stablehand came through the house door in a flat-out dive to smother Rob.

Tim shot at June, missed, and made the only move left him. He dived flat on his belly and rolled; hearing Roy land on Rob and Rob's cry of surprise and pain, as June shot again.

Tim felt the sting of flying gravel on his cheek, nothing more. Now he was on his belly, facing June again. Rob and the stablehand were wrestling almost at June's feet. June was levering a shell into his gun, backing away from the wrestlers.

Taking quick and careful sight now, his left hand

cradling his right wrist, Tim fired. June vanished behind the wrestlers.

Tim rose, crouching low, and ran. He was even with them when he halted abruptly. June lay on his belly, the back of his head gone, a grayish bloody smear where it had been.

Abruptly, Roy ran past him heading for June and the rifle beside him. Tim moved quickly toward June, but Roy led him by a pace. He was bending over, reaching for the rifle, when Tim's foot stomped down on it. For three savage seconds, Roy tried to yank the rifle from under Tim's boot and then he gave up.

He rose and Tim saw he was crying. "You son of a bitch! He was my friend!"

"Back off," Tim ordered quietly.

The young man obeyed and Tim was bent over, picking up the rifle, when Beth came running out of the house. She ran straight for Rob, who was just getting to his feet. She came into his arms. "Are you all right, Rob? Are you hurt?"

"Just mussed up," Rob said, patting her back.

Now Beth broke away from him and ran the few feet to Tim. She threw her arms around him, holding him fiercely, and buried her head in his chest. She was sobbing now, saying brokenly over and over, "Thank God, thank God, you're safe!"

Rifle still in one hand, Tim hugged her to him. "Easy girl, easy. It's over."

As he hugged her to him, he saw Norah come out of the house. She walked over to June, looked, turned her head away, then reached behind her, untied her apron, and spread it over June's upper body. Her cheeks were wet with tears as she turned and went back into the house.

Now the curious began to gather—Dad, the clerk, two men and three women, and Rob started to answer their questions. Tim took Beth's arm and they moved into the house's big kitchen. The bedroom door was closed and they could hear Norah sobbing behind it.

Tim put the carbine on the nearest table while Beth crossed to the sink to wash her tear-stained face. When she was finished, she came back to Tim who, still standing, was counting out coins from a snap purse and laying them on the table.

Beth came up beside him and said, "What on earth are you doing, Tim?"

Tim didn't look at her as he put down another coin, saying, "Paying back the money you loaned me, my hospital bill, and Rob's bill."

"But—what's the hurry, Tim? We can do that at home."

Tim finished, pocketed his purse, then reached out, put a hand on her slim shoulder and said, "Sit down, Beth."

She seated herself on the bench, puzzled. Tim eased himself half onto the table, one leg bracing himself, the other dangling. He said then, "I'm not going back to Driscoll, Beth. You and Rob can take the noon stage back. I'm headed for Corbett and a northbound train."

Beth watched him closely, and finally said with open bitterness, "What a hell of a way to say good-bye, Tim. What a hell of a place to say it in."

"None better." He gestured toward the window. "See that tall man out there."

Beth didn't even look. "Rob, you mean."

Tim nodded. "He loves you, Beth. So do I—too much to ask you to marry me."

Beth was silent a moment, looking up at him. "What on earth does that mean?"

"You watched what happened out there ten minutes ago?"

"Every hideous second of it," Beth said in a low voice.

"Enjoy it?"

"I hated it!"

"That's what I mean," Tim said quietly. "That's my work, my life. If it hadn't been for Rob ramming out there and shaking up June, it might have gone the other way. It might go the other way next time. It might—"

Beth came to her feet and Tim rose. Beth ran into his enfolding arms.

She talked into his chest. "I haven't any words to thank you, Tim. I—"

"Hush," Tim said. He reached down, tilted her face up, and kissed her. "That's for unscrambling my head. For more, too."

He left, and Beth moved to the window, an overwhelming sadness in her. She saw Tim move among the people, stop beside Rob, talk with him for a moment, and then the two men—her men—shook hands. Afterward, she watched Tim's broad back as he headed for the road and walked out of her line of sight. She was crying, but she was happy.

ABOUT THE AUTHOR

LUKE SHORT, whose real name is Frederick D. Glidden, was born in Illinois in 1907. Before devoting himself to writing westerns, he was a trapper in the Canadian Sub-arctic, worked as an assistant to an archeologist, and was a newsman. He believes an author can write best about the places he knows most intimately, so he usually locates his westerns on familiar ground. He is an avid skier and mountain explorer, and now lives with his wife in Aspen, Colorado.

LUKE SHORT
TODAY'S BEST-SELLING WESTERN WRITER

RELAX!
SIT DOWN
and Catch Up On Your Reading!

Ross Macdonald

The New #1 Detective Novelist In America

Lew Archer Novels

"The finest series of detective novels ever written by an American . . . I have been reading him for years and he has yet to disappoint. Classify him how you will, he is one of the best novelists now operating, and all he does is keep on getting better."

—The New York Times

☐ THE UNDERGROUND MAN	Q7040	$1.25
☐ THE WAY SOME PEOPLE DIE	N6747	95¢
☐ THE ZEBRA-STRIPED HEARSE	N6791	95¢
☐ THE CHILL	N6792	95¢
☐ THE MOVING TARGET	N6793	95¢
☐ THE DROWNING POOL	N6794	95¢
☐ THE FAR SIDE OF THE DOLLAR	N6795	95¢
☐ THE GALTON CASE	N6796	95¢
☐ THE INSTANT ENEMY	N6797	95¢
☐ THE FERGUSON AFFAIR	N6798	95¢
☐ THE GOODBYE LOOK	N5357	95¢
☐ THE NAME IS ARCHER	N5996	95¢

Buy them at your local bookstore or use this handy coupon for ordering: